Pomegranate and T

Edogawa Ranpo

Translated from the Japanese by Alexis J Brown
All rights reserved Zakuro Books

Pomegranate

(石榴)

1

It has been my habit for some time to keep a 'Crime Journal' comprehensively recording the details of every notable case I have been involved in during my extensive career as a police detective. Although oddly enough I never came to record the events I intend to transcribe here - namely the 'Case of the Acid Murderer' - despite it being a rather bizarre and fascinating tale. I must have simply forgotten this peculiar episode among the numerous cases I have worked on. It only happened recently that a chance event caused me to recall this episode in full. This "chance event" led to a quite shocking conclusion, but I will come to that soon enough, let me say for now that what initially stirred my memory was the appearance of a gentleman by the name of Inomata whose acquaintance I made at the S- hot spring resort in Nagano Prefecture. Or rather, a copy of an English detective story which that gentleman was carrying. What grave significance that book seems to hold for me now as I think back to its grimy, blackened cloth cover.

At the time of writing these words it is early autumn, 19--. One month previous to this, to escape the summer heat, I visited the S- hot spring resort deep in the mountains of Shinano Province. The resort is located in an extremely remote part of the country. First I had to journey to Y- Station on the Shinetsu Line, then change to a private railway, and from the last stop on this line take a rickety bus ride for two uncomfortable hours. The hotel I stayed in had rather inadequate facilities; the food was unpleasant; and there was little there to keep me amused; but as an out-of-the-way mountain retreat it was irreproachable. Roughly 350 yards from my hotel was a deep gorge where a splendid waterfall could be found, and from the nearby surrounding mountains wild boar sometimes appeared - it was even said they ventured close to the gardens behind the hotel.

The name of the place was the Suiranso Grand, which even though being the most salubrious looking lodgings at the resort was "Grand" in name alone. The Suiranso had a distinctly provincial air; although fairly spacious, the building itself was in the style of an old, dingy mountain villa; the housemaids wore clumsily applied face powder; the summer kimonos provided for guests were short and stiff with starch. But despite being so far off the beaten track the hotel was near full - it was the height of the season after all - with many guests coming from major cities such as Tokyo and Nagoya. The gentleman I mentioned earlier, Inomata, was one such guest, a stockbroker based in the capital.

Now, as well as being a police detective by trade, I am also an avid reader of detective novels. In fact in my case it was the excitement I enjoyed from reading of criminal cases in such works that led to me joining the service in the first place - working my way up from local constable to an investigator in the Tokyo Police Department - so that finally I have ended up dedicating half my life to criminal investigation. It is because of this rather eccentric pastime of mine that whenever I stay at a health spa or some such place, rather than remaining vigilant for any suspicious characters among my fellow guests, I am instead always on the lookout for any other lovers of detective fiction -

someone who I can debate the relative merits of the genre with. At this moment in Japan, although detective stories are very popular, people mostly read them in weekly magazines, so you rarely see anyone walk around with an actual copy of a published book in their hand. This has always left me feeling somewhat disappointed, but the day I came to stay at the Suiranso Grand, I ran into exactly the kind of person I had been hoping to meet. This in fact was Inomata.

Although at first I took this gentleman to be younger than me, I later came to discover he was actually 44 years of age, five years my senior, and also a rare enthusiast of the detective genre. His suitcase was filled with such novels, and furthermore, most of them English translations. He caught my eye as he sat reading one such story in a wicker armchair on the second floor balcony of the hotel. Without either of us making a direct approach, we happened to fall into conversation, and by the following day had become quite well acquainted.

There was something about Inomata's physical appearance that was strangely appealing. Although he was not that old, his well-shaped head was as hairless as a hen egg; his eyebrows were thin, but graceful; he wore round yellow-tinted rimless glasses behind which could be seen a pair of double lidded oval-shaped eyes; his nose was slender and Roman; he had a short moustache and beautifully trimmed sideburns that came down to the point of his chin. He was somehow Western in looks, and remarkably handsome. Despite being dressed in one of the ill-fitting hotel kimonos - sitting neatly with his knees together, his sash tied in a precise manner around his waist - his upright posture was much more like that of a sober university professor than of a stockbroker.

I soon came to learn that Inomata's wife had recently passed away. The great sadness he felt for this woman, whom he must have loved very dearly, was clearly etched into the elegant brow of his pale face. It also seemed that his beloved detective stories did little to distract him from his grief. I observed how he spent most of his time shut away in his room, half read books lying on the tatami mats around him, as he sat resting his chin in his hand, staring with a vacant expression past the balcony at the green mountains rising up in the distance - a figure seemingly so deep in melancholy.

One afternoon, two days after I arrived at the Suiranso, I decided to go for a stroll following lunch. Dressed in a thin kimono and wearing a pair of wooden clogs branded with the hotel's name, I left by a rear gate and headed for a park-like wooded area called Suiran Gardens. On the way, I happened to catch sight of Inomata, also in a kimono, leaning against a Chinkapin tree, of course immersed in a book. Instinctively I went towards him wondering what he was reading that day and whether indeed it was another detective novel. When I called out, Inomata sharply raised his head, then after smiling and greeting me he held up the bluish black cover of his book and showed me the golden lettering on its spine. Emblazoned in large Gothic print were the words: "TRENT'S LAST CASE   E.C. BENTLEY". He then folded the corner of the page he'd been reading and while playfully turning the volume over in his hands, began to speak with great enthusiasm: "Of course I expect you will have read this yourself. For me, this is already my fifth time - look, see how dog-eared it has become! It's a truly wonderful work of fiction - perhaps one of the few great masterpieces of the genre."

"Bentley? Yes I read this quite some time ago," I replied. "I've mostly forgotten the details, but I recall reading in a literary magazine somewhere that this, and 'The Cask' by Freeman Wills Crofts, were perhaps the two greatest English detective novels of the day." For a while we went on to discuss the ins and outs of the genre, then all of a sudden Inomata, who was aware of my profession, turned to me and said: "I'm sure you've been involved in many strange cases in your time. I often make clippings of the popular crime stories that the press make so much of, and apply my own amateur reasoning to them, but I imagine there are some interesting cases that don't make it into the papers. I wonder if you've handled any such peculiar episodes someone like me would not have heard of? Of course you would not be able to talk of anything recent, but perhaps an old case long forgotten..."

This was a question I'm often asked by new acquaintances of mine who share my love of detective fiction. I replied: "Ah well, I usually record my noteworthy cases in a journal, but such crimes are always covered in detail by the press at the time, so are not so unusual I think..." But as I spoke these words I happened to look down at the book Inomata was still turning around in his hands, and in that moment the case I mentioned earlier leapt into my mind, just as the full moon can suddenly emerge from out of a murky night sky. I continued: "In reality the number of criminal cases that can be solved through pure reasoning is very small. This is why true crime is often rather dull for lovers of detective fiction. Rather than deduction, chance and legwork play a much more important role. The work of Crofts gives a better sense of this reality. His novels are of the procedural type of detective fiction - his detectives solve their cases by meticulously carrying out routine investigations, rather than through any cerebral exercise. However, this is not to say there aren't exceptions. In fact an odd episode from around ten years ago has just occurred to me - let's call it the 'Case of the Acid Murderer' - as far as I remember this was a local affair so mostly not covered by the papers in Tokyo and Osaka, but nevertheless a rather interesting turn of events. It happened so long ago, I hadn't thought of it at all until speaking with you just now. If you don't mind, perhaps I could relate this tale to you?"

"Yes, please do" Inomata replied, almost losing his footing with excitement, his eyes shining with childlike anticipation, "I'd like to know as much detail as possible. Just hearing such a title makes it sound utterly fascinating.

"Although, standing here...it's perhaps not the best location. It would be better if we found somewhere we can take our time and feel at ease. Then again, the hotel can be quite noisy during the afternoon. I wonder, if we follow that path towards the waterfall, I believe there is a spot on the way that would suit us well..."

Hearing Inomata speak, my own enthusiasm grew. It's an odd habit of mine that when I am about to record a case in my 'Crime Journal', I first tell it in some detail to an acquaintance. In doing so, as I speak, dim recollections gradually sharpen, and the story as a whole becomes more cohesive. This is most useful when it comes to the actual writing stage. I also take some pride in my skill as a storyteller, and enjoy arranging the facts of a case like that of a detective novel to make it as interesting as possible for the listener. I felt today I could speak especially well, so was also filled with a childlike excitement, and readily accepted Inomata's request.

The path we climbed was half covered in weeds and meandered off to the left and right. After about a hundred yards Inomata, who was ahead of me, suddenly stopped and made an indication that this was the place. It certainly was a marvellous location. On one side was a steep mountain slope, dense with vegetation. The other side looked over the sheer drop of a deep gorge, reaching down countless yards. At its base an eerie silence emanated from a pitch-black pool of water. Deviating a little from the narrow path was a large boulder which peered over the chasm like the eaves of a house. On top of this rock was a flat space about the size of one tatami mat.

"Isn't this the perfect setting for your tale? A ravine edge where one slip means certain death – it's exactly the spot for a detective story I think. There's something most suitable about using a rock which makes your skin itch just to sit on it, as the place to hear of some dreadful murder, don't you agree?"

Inomata spoke with evident glee, then suddenly clambered up the boulder and planted himself down on a spot immediately overlooking the gorge.

"It's certainly a fearsome location. I'm glad you're not of a villainous nature or I wouldn't wish to sit anywhere near you", I said smiling, taking up a place next to him.

The sky above us was overcast and grey. Somehow, although it was cool, the atmosphere caused me to break into a sweat. The mountains on the other side of the gorge were dark and foreboding, and there was no sign of any other living creature as far as the eye could see. Even the constant cacophony of birdsong was now somehow subdued, and hardly a note could be heard. Only the faint rumbling of a waterfall from a river that couldn't be seen reverberated in the air. As Inomata had said, it was the ideal setting for my peculiar tale. So at last, eager to begin, I started to relate the 'Case of the Acid Murderer'.

2

It was ten years ago in the autumn of 19-- in a newly developed suburban district of Nagoya called town G. Nowadays town G, like the rest of the city, is a lively location, its streets are lined with shops and family homes, but back then, ten years ago, it was a rather desolate place. There were more empty lots than there were buildings, and it became so dark at night most people would walk around with a torch.

Late one evening a policeman assigned to the local station was on patrol in this lonely neighbourhood, when he happened to notice something rather strange. A reddish light coming from a house that should have been empty – a house that stood alone in the middle of some vacant land; a derelict rundown place that had had its shutters closed for about a year; a house that couldn't possibly have had a tenant move in so quickly. And what was more, something seemed to be squirming around in front of this dim light. The fact that light was visible at all meant the shutters had been opened. But who on earth had opened them? And what were they doing trespassing in this derelict building? The policeman's suspicions were thoroughly aroused. He moved closer, walking softly to conceal the sound of his footsteps, then peered in through the half opened front door. The first thing he noticed was what seemed like a crate for oranges had been placed upside down on the dusty wooden floor with a single large candle on top of it. In front of this candle was a dark object like a stepladder, standing with its legs opened out, and low down in front of this was a silhouette shifting about restlessly. On closer inspection though, the stepladder turned out to be an artist's easel with a canvas, and the shadow, a young man with long hair earnestly moving a paintbrush.

But how outrageous! For a student to break into an empty house on a whim, and paint by candlelight. And what on earth was he painting? At such a late hour by such a deliberately dim glow?

The policeman stared intently at whatever was on the other side of the crate. He could just make out the artist's model – a shape stretched out on the dusty floor. But as his view was obscured he couldn't immediately grasp the true nature of what was lying there. By extending his back to peer over the shadow of the crate however he saw that whatever it was, it was wearing clothes, though somehow it did not seem human. He later described it as like a pomegranate that had burst apart, a truly terrible and mysterious sight. When I saw for myself, I also couldn't help think of this fruit, squashed and bruised when overripe - a monstrous, succulent pomegranate, its insides split open, lying prone on the ground dressed in a dark kimono.

Of course you will have understood by now, this was indeed a human being, though it was certainly hard to tell, and one whose pitiful face was a mess of open wounds and weeping sores, smeared with blood.

Because the young artist seemed so strangely calm and enraptured as he painted, at first the policeman wondered if his "model" was wearing some kind of grotesque and freakish make up. After all he thought, art students tended to involve themselves in such bizarre activities. However, even if it was just a costume there was no reason to stand by idly. This youth had brazenly broken into someone else's house. But when questioned, the peculiar long-haired artist displayed no sign of being flustered. On the contrary he turned on the policeman, accusing him of "getting in his way" and disturbing his "moment of inspiration". Paying no heed to this the officer moved closer to investigate the horror lying on the other side of the crate, and it was then he confirmed this was no model wearing make-up. This was the body of a man. A man killed in such a monstrous way his appearance was almost too terrible to gaze upon.

Without another word the policeman - sensing this was a major case and thrilled he'd finally landed the big catch he'd secretly been hoping for - marched the young artist back to the neighbourhood police box. He then made an excited call to the main station seeking assistance. You may already have guessed who answered that call; it was none other than myself of course, at that time a rookie detective assigned to M district in my home town of Nagoya.

It was a little after nine when I picked up the receiver and apart from those of us on the night shift everyone had already gone home for the day. After some time and effort I managed to get through to the public prosecutor's office and the city headquarters. It was eventually decided the station chief himself would attend, along with myself and another veteran detective. We all left together to make a detailed examination of the crime scene.

According to the police doctor the victim was male, previously of good health, and aged between 34 and 35. He was of average height and build with no distinguishing features. He wore no shirt, but a plain silk robe under a dull-coloured patterned kimono with an informal silk sash. The kimono was shabby and worn, so it seemed he had not occupied a high position in society, at least at the time of his death. Both hands and feet had been tied together with rough rope, but before being tied up it seemed he had resisted strongly. There were several scratch marks along his chest and both arms. There could be no doubt he had put up quite a fight - but why had no-one heard this and made a call to the police? Well as I said before, the house was on vacant land, it stood alone in the middle of a wide open lot, some distance away from any other buildings.

So then, hands and feet tied, face sprayed with a corrosive substance. Talking of this gruesome matter now brings it back to me so vividly - I feel I could describe every tiny detail of that unearthly scene. But...well, perhaps you would tire of such an account. Instead, let me move on to the cause of death. Now, however much the victim had been splashed with what appeared to be sulphuric acid, it was concluded that the burns on his face would not have killed him. The police doctor looked for any signs the man had been struck or throttled before the liquid had done its damage, but apart from the relatively minor scratches to his body there was no trace of any other injury. Finally though, he came to understand the truly awful nature of the crime.

"It seems spraying acid on the face of his victim was not the culprit's primary intention", he said turning to us, "you might say these terrible burns are in fact just an accidental by-product of his real aim...instead, gentlemen, please examine the inside of the victim's mouth." So saying, he pulled back the man's lips with a pair of tweezers and allowed us to peer inside. Here was a sight even more horrific than that of the poor man's face. The doctor continued: "I can't be certain but judging by the stains on the wooden floor it seems the victim vomited a great deal of acid before death. Since the substance would not have entered his mouth and reached his stomach simply from being splashed on his face, it is quite clear that he'd been forced to drink it. Most likely his hands and feet first tied, then his nose held shut. I don't think we can draw any other conclusion."

Well...what a truly horrific notion - but no matter how horrific, it appeared the doctor's prognosis was accurate. The following day an autopsy of the body confirmed it. Surely, to commit murder by forcing your victim to drink sulphuric acid was an act of unconscionable madness. The work of some lunatic. If not, the killer must have harboured such a deep grudge or terrible animosity towards the victim, that to simply kill him was not enough, they had to conjure up something so outrageously cruel (as for the time of death, the doctor could not of course say precisely, but he estimated it was some time in the late afternoon or early evening of that day, perhaps between four and six o'clock).

We now mostly understood the method, but when it came to who the murderer was, why they did it, and who they killed, it may sound strange to say but we hadn't the slightest clue. Of course the long-haired young artist was detained at the main station and ferociously interrogated, but he insisted he was innocent and had no idea who the victim was - and never at any time diverged from his story.

The young man was called Akaike, and he was indeed a student, enrolled at a fairly large private school of western art - the name of which he gave - and that he rented a room in a neighbouring district of town G.

What kind of person doesn't immediately call the police when they come across a body? And then, how on earth can someone calmly sit there and produce a painting of such a dreadful corpse? What possible excuse can they have, other than they themselves are the killer?

When these questions were put to the young man, he replied in the following way: "For quite a while I'd been drawn to that derelict building. It has the air of a haunted house, and I'd been inside many times. All the locks were broken so anyone could go in if they wanted. I loved spending time there in the darkness, lost in my own imaginings. That was my intention that night too, but when I got inside, there right before my eyes lying on the floor was a body. It was already quite dark so I lit a match to get a better view - and what an amazing sight it was. This was exactly the subject I'd been dreaming about for so long. In the pitch black, the artistic power of human flesh dazzled at me like a blood red flower. How much had I longed for this! I could not have wished for a better model. I rushed home to collect my painting materials, canvas, and candles and was completely engrossed in the movement of my brush, capturing that image, until that hateful policeman came and interrupted me."

I find it hard to describe, but listening to Akaike was like hearing the madly impassioned song of a demon. He did not appear completely insane, but there was something abnormal in his nature. At the very least he certainly suffered from a kind of pathological condition. Such a person couldn't be judged by normal standards. Even though he gave the impression he was telling the truth, it was difficult to make any kind of conjecture from his testimony. It did seem though that anyone who could gaze on such a bloody corpse and so calmly sit down and paint, could also be capable of murder. This was the general view, and the station chief was especially certain Akaike was our man. Even though his story held up there was no chance of his release and he was kept locked in his cell and put through an intense interrogation.

Two days passed in this way. I myself, in the manner of so many fictional detectives, had already crept around the floor of that derelict house and the ground outside like a trained bloodhound, but had found no container of sulphuric acid, nor any fingerprints or footprints – in fact not one single tangible clue. I questioned every neighbour and nearby resident, but to no avail - at any rate the nearest house was over 60 yards away. While at the same time, Akaike, our one and only suspect was allowed hardly a wink of sleep over two nights of persistent questioning. But the more he was accused, the more frenzied his responses became, and no breakthrough came. More than anything though, our biggest problem was we still had no idea who the victim was. With his disfigured face and no other distinguishing features, our only hope was if someone recognised the pattern of his kimono. This was all we had to go on. We first tried the barbershop owner who rented Akaike his room, but he told us he'd no recollection of it at all. There was also no clear answer from any of the locals. We'd finally hit a brick wall. But then, on the evening of the investigation's third day, the victim's identity unexpectedly came to light - and through a peculiar source. It turned out that this man whose life had come to such a cruel end - although rather down on his luck in the months before his death - was at one time the respectable owner of a long-established family store.

And it is here my story slowly transforms into that of a detective novel.

That evening I had remained at the station house for a meeting to discuss the case. At about eight o'clock I received a phone call from Kinuyo Tanimura, the wife of an acquaintance of mine. She implored me to visit her at once as she had a private matter to discuss urgently. It was in fact in connection to the "acid murder" that everybody had been talking about. But she begged me not to tell my colleagues where I was going until I had heard her story. Her voice was oddly strained, and she seemed extremely agitated.

I'm sure you have heard of Tanimura, for this is the name of a large confectionery store that sells Nagoya's famous speciality - *Mujina* rice cakes. It is a long running family business known by everyone in the region with a history going back to the Edo era, and stands in comparison to some of Tokyo's finest establishments such as Fugetsu-Do and Toraya. *Mujina*, which is an old term for a racoon, may be an odd thing to call a sweet, but there is an elaborate story behind it going back many years so the people of the area do not think it strange at all. I myself was friends with the owner of Tanimura, a gentleman called Man'emon. Now, although "Man'emon" makes him sound like an old man, the name was actually a Tanimura family tradition passed down through the generations, and at that time he was only around 33 or 34 years of age. Man'emon was a respectable, university educated, bright young man who dabbled somewhat in literature, so for a lover of novels like myself, he made for an excellent partner in conversation...ah, and now I come to think of it, we even debated the finer points of detective stories as well. Kinuyo was Man'emon's beautiful young wife, and I could not possibly disregard such a phone call from her. I made up some excuse, left the meeting, and rushed over to the Tanimura's residence.

Their shop selling the famous *Mujina* rice cakes was on T street, Nagoya's main thoroughfare, in an old fashioned warehouse, but the family themselves lived out of town within the jurisdiction of M station. It was not far away so I went there on foot, and as I hurriedly strode down the darkened streets, I suddenly looked up and realised, the derelict house at the centre of this perplexing case was itself only a stone's throw from the Tanimura's home. A distance of perhaps only 350 yards. With such a geographical connection, Kinuyo's words over the telephone began to take on a rather deeper significance.

Kinuyo normally had a healthy complexion, but that night her face was as white as a sheet. She was terribly ill at ease, and the instant she saw me she almost clung to my sleeve, pleading with me for advice. When I asked what on earth had happened, she replied that her husband, Man'emon, had disappeared. On the morning after the discovery of the body at the derelict house, Man'emon had left for Tokyo on the 4.40 a.m. train in order to meet with the executive of a sugar manufacturer in regards to some interest he had with setting up a new confectionery company. At that time there was no express service, so if you wished to arrive at Tokyo Station for just after lunch you had to leave at the crack of dawn. She assured me he left that morning from the house they shared together on the outskirts of Nagoya. The day before, he had stayed in his study late into the night, researching material for this enterprise. However, the day he left, Kinuyo received a call from the sugar manufacturer to say Man'emon had not arrived for his meeting. They asked whether he had been delayed in some way. It seemed the matter was rather urgent and they were getting impatient. Kinuyo, surprised by the call, replied that she was certain her husband had taken the train that morning and that he would not have stopped anywhere on the way. The person on the other end of the line went on to say they had even called Mane'mon's regular hotel in Akasaka, but it seemed he had not arrived there either. It was unlikely Man'emon would have decided to stay anywhere else and it all appeared a little strange. The phone call then ended without anything being settled.

All of the next next day, that is to say up until she called me at the station that evening, Kinuyo checked several times with hotels in Tokyo, friends, customers in Shizuoka, and of course the sugar manufacturer, any place she could think of to see if they knew of Man'emon's whereabouts. But nobody had seen him. He had been missing now for two whole days. Under normal circumstances Kinuyo said she would not have felt so worried, but then after hearing about what happened the night before he left...she somehow felt a terrible foreboding.

It seemed to me Kinuyo was holding something back. She referred of course to the acid murder - was it possible she might have some idea who the victim was? Somehow I instinctively felt this to be true, and tentatively put the question to her.

"Yes...", she responded hesitantly, "the truth is, ever since I saw that night's evening edition, I knew. But I was so scared, I couldn't bring myself to call the police..."

"Who?" I blurted out, "I mean, the man killed in that derelict house, who was he?"

Kinuyo continued: "There was, you see, this shop owner, our rival for many years whose store also sold *Mujina* rice cakes. His name was Shuichi Kotono. He wore a kimono just like the one described in the newspaper. But that is not all, in truth there is something even more conclusive."

On hearing this, I immediately understood why Kinuyo had been reluctant to reveal who the victim was until now, and why, even though she was sick with worry, she'd not reported Man'emon's disappearance. It all clicked in my mind. Kinuyo harboured a terrible suspicion.

You see, once there were indeed two stores in Nagoya that sold *Mujina* rice cakes. Both of them in the centre of town, almost side by side on the main thoroughfare. One, as I said, run by my friend Man'emon Tanimura, Kinuyo's husband. The other by Shuichi Kotono. Both were well established emporiums going back generations, and both claimed to be the first to produce this local speciality. They maintained a bitter rivalry, each with a large gold-lettered sign outside their premises proclaiming them to be the "Original home of the *Mujina* rice cake".

Because of this rivalry it goes without saying the relationship between the two families was hardly harmonious, in fact their mutual ill-will over a confectionery product was really quite extraordinary. Going back several generations, stories of the feud were legendary. There were tales of workers for the Kotono family sneaking into the Tanimura workshop and mixing sand in with their rice cakes; and of the Tanimura family hiring a priest to pray for the Kotono family's downfall; and of a fist fight in the middle of town between several dozen workers from both families in which much blood was shed; and of Man'emon's great grandfather drawing swords and duelling in the street with the head of the Kotono family at that time like two samurai. There were countless incidents. A truly terrible animosity had been nurtured across several generations. This bad blood must still have inflamed the hearts of Man'emon and Kotono, as the feud between the two families only intensified even more it seems.

When they were children, Man'emon and Kotono went to the same elementary school - although in different classes - and every time they ran across each other in the playground, or to and from school, there would be a fight. Their scuffles often resulting in blood being drawn. Over the years this conflict continued to take many forms, and eventually the pair quarrelled even in matters of love. That is to say, Man'emon and Kotono fell for the same girl. After a rather convoluted series of events Man'emon eventually won the girl's heart, claimed victory in this particular battle, and around three years before the acid murder case the couple were married in a magnificent ceremony. His new bride was of course Kinuyo.

This defeat would prove to be the ruin of the Kotono family. Shuichi truly loved Kinuyo, her rejection left him caring for nothing. He neglected his duties at the shop and instead frequented the pleasure quarters of the city. Not only this, the business became the target of intense pressure from a large-scale confectionery manufacturer which already had a site next door, and soon enough, Kotono's store went under. This long standing establishment, with a history going back to Edo times, just like that, simply slipped into another's hands.

Around the time of the shop's bankruptcy Kotono's parents died, and because he had remained single he had no children and was now completely alone. He scratched a living with the help of relatives, but his behaviour grew more mean spirited, he lost any sense of shame and cared not for his reputation. He went around his former suppliers looking for charity, and even frequently visited the residence of his old enemy Man'emon, crawling home after being treated to some dinner. After a while, since Kotono acted so meek and humble, Man'emon softened to him, even treating him like a friend, but he soon realized the real reason behind Kotono's visits - it was only to gaze upon Kinuyo's remarkable beauty and hear her sweet voice. At length, Kinuyo herself asked if Man'emon could stop Kotono from visiting as she felt some uneasiness, so one day Man'emon and Kotono got into a furious argument, even trading blows. After that Kotono never again set foot in the Tanimura's home. At about the same time certain scurrilous rumours regarding Man'emon and his wife began to circulate. The most awful of these cast doubt on Kinuyo's virtue. And what's more, according to the story being spread around, the other party involved was none other than Kotono himself (even though Man'emon knew these stories were compete fabrications, when he came to hear about them indirectly it seemed he couldn't help harbouring a strange suspicion about his wife; my own wife often visited Kinuyo at this time and heard how the couple's relationship had become very strained).

In this way the ancestral hatred and bad blood between Man'emon and Kotono apparently grew more ferocious, welling up inside them both, finally leading to a flurry of provocative letters from Kotono filled with curses arriving at Man'emon's door. Now ordinarily Man'emon was a reasonable gentleman of good character, but he did possess a temper, and could fly into a devilish rage over any small mishap. This perhaps being the legacy of the combative Tanimura blood in his veins.

The acid murder case occurred just as this situation reached, as it were, boiling point, so it was only natural that Kinuyo should feel such a sickening dread. On the morning after Kotono was killed by an act of unparalleled cruelty, her husband had boarded a train for Tokyo and simply vanished.

Now, let me return to that evening when I was called to Kinuyo's home and she told me she was sure it was Shuichi Kotono who'd been murdered in that derelict house. Not only did Kotono's kimono match that of the victim's, Kinuyo had further proof, and so saying she took out a scrap of tightly folded paper from beneath her sash and opened it to show me. It turned out to be a letter, dated with the same day and month as the murder - I don't recall the exact date - the contents being as follows: "I shall be waiting for you at 4 o'clock at that empty house in town G and hope you will come and meet me there. [Since the letter simply said "that" empty house, Man'emon, for it was he who'd received the letter, must already have known the whereabouts of the property]. There we can hopefully bury our past differences. You won't be too afraid to face me I'm sure." Such was the rather solemn message. It was signed of course by Shuichi Kotono, and at the bottom of the page was an imprint of his shop's trademark.

"And so," I asked, "did your husband in fact go to the house?" Man'emon was certainly the kind of person to do so reckless a thing when his blood was up.

"That I cannot say. When he saw this letter his complexion darkened, and as was his habit - perhaps you have seen this for yourself - the vein on his temple began to throb. I was deeply concerned. I told him it was best not to meddle with someone so apparently out of his mind, and urged him not to go, but..." Kinuyo was initially relieved that Man'emon appeared to shut himself away in his study that day from lunch until late into the night, working on the new business proposal to take to Tokyo. But thinking about it later...well, he was not the sort of person to venture out, even for one evening, without saying where he was going, so to disappear for two whole days? Kinuyo's initial relief came from knowing her husband had not left the house, but in truth his study faced the rear garden, and he could quite freely have climbed down from the verandah and exited via the back gate. A distrustful person might have concluded it was not out of the question for him to have slipped out that night to the nearby derelict house and then casually return to his study without any of the household noticing.

What was hard to believe was that Man'emon had gone with the intention of killing. There was no reason for him to discard everything he had, his family's good name, his beautiful bride, just to take Kotono's wretched life. Assuming he did go to that house, he most likely went simply to rebuke Kotono for his vile behaviour, and settle things with his fists. But as I said, the person lying in wait for him was by now a cursed figure close to madness, and who knew what scheme he had concocted. Perhaps Kotono himself had brought the bottle of sulphuric acid, and was preparing to disfigure the other's face...this was of course only supposition, but nevertheless a very reasonable hypothesis don't you think? In Kotono's eyes Man'emon was a love rival, one he detested more than anything in this world. And what better revenge to take on your rival than leave them with the hideous appearance of a leper. Not only could he deface the man who had stolen his love, and have him spend the rest of his life in agony, but also the women who rejected him would forever have to tend to her husband's every need - in effect with one act Kotono could take retribution on them both.

But once Man'emon had entered that house and seen through Kotono's plan, what happened then? Would he have been able to restrain his explosive temper? Did the venomous hatred that had festered in his blood over generations cause him to lose all reason, and rage like a wild beast? It is not hard to imagine the appalling struggle that could have taken place. And in that moment could he have snatched the acid prepared by his opponent and use it against him, bringing about such terrible results? None of this was beyond the bounds of conjecture.

Kinuyo had not slept a wink since the night before as this awful fantasy kept playing out in her mind. Finally she could stand it no more, and had called me at the station and revealed her dreadful suspicion.

"But no matter how enraged Man'emon was, could he really have committed such an act? Perhaps you don't yet know, but the acid wasn't only poured over the victim, he had also been forced to drink it. It used to be that criminals had molten lead dripped over cuts in their back as punishment, but the atrocious crime committed in that derelict house was surely just as sadistic. Could your husband really have been so cruel?"

I spoke these words without thinking, but when I had finished Kinuyo glanced upwards at me uncomfortably, her face suddenly flushed bright red, and I instantly knew the truth of it. Man'emon did indeed have a brutish side to him. Not so long ago my wife had accompanied Kinuyo to a hot spring resort in Kasagi, and while there, she noticed several strange red marks all over her body. Kinuyo spoke only to my wife about the marks and saying no more forbid her to tell another soul, but there could be no doubt, her husband had a sadistic streak and this is what had made Kinuyo blush. I acted as if I hadn't noticed however, and instead continued by offering some words of comfort: "I'm sure you're worrying over nothing. There's sure to be some reasonable explanation for all of this. After all it's only been two days since Man'emon went away, we don't yet know if he is actually missing. And even if Kotono is the victim, we currently have in custody a seemingly disturbed young man by the name of Akaike who was found painting a picture at the scene, and unless we find any evidence to the contrary he remains our number one suspect."

I tried consoling Kinuyo in this way, and although on the surface she seemed to accept my words, I also intuitively felt she did not believe me for a moment. "There's no use causing a fuss," I went on, "I won't breathe a word of this to anyone. Let's wait one or two days and see what happens. Why I bet at any moment Man'emon will simply walk in through that door – however – on the question of the victim being Shuichi Kotono, as a police officer I can't simply let that go. But you or your husband's names don't have to come into it, there are plenty of other sources I can confirm this from, so you needn't worry." So saying, I left Kinuyo that evening. Of course, based on the knowledge that Kotono was indeed the victim, my first intention was to visit his humble lodgings and ascertain if he was really missing or not. But when I got back to the station the place seemed alive with activity. Something must have happened while I was away. Chief Inspector Saito – at that time one of the prefecture's most eminent detectives – suddenly slapped me on the back and exclaimed, "Hey, we got a lead on the body!"

It turned out that shortly after I left the meeting that evening, two sweet shop owners had come to the station and asked to see the kimono worn by the victim in the "acid murder case". Fortunately the kimono was still in the evidence room, and as soon as the two gentlemen laid eyes on it, they looked at each other and nodded. "That's Shuichi Kotono's, who used to run the *Mujina* rice cake shop. No doubt about it," they said. "When Shuichi was in his prime he ordered that pattern especially from the tailors. There's not two kimonos like it in all of Nagoya. What's more, he even wore it recently when he came to our shop. It's Shuichi's without question." Such was the certainty of their testimony. An officer from the station was dispatched to Kotono's address to investigate his whereabouts, and sure enough, it turned out Kotono had left the day before yesterday and had not yet returned home. There could be no mistake. The man killed in that derelict house was Shuichi Kotono. Kinuyo's instincts had proved right, at least in regards to the identity of the victim. I couldn't help tremble with a terrible feeling of dread that the culprit was also as she had surmised.

"Now we know Kotono is the victim, we'll need to investigate that other *Mujina* shop, after all they had quite a famous rivalry. Let's see, what was its name, oh yes, Tanimura. You're pals with the owner there aren't you? That puts you in a bit of a spot eh?"

I jumped at the Chief Inspector's words. "Me? Not at all, I..."

"Hah, well police work is tricky when friends are involved," the great detective said rather gleefully, "right, I'd better take the lead on this one. Let's see if I can't sniff out the solution to this mystery myself."

Chief Inspector Saito moved the investigation forward in the brisk and businesslike manner you'd expect from such a well respected detective. By the end of that evening he'd learned of Man'emon's disappearance, and the next day he and several junior officers called on the Tanimura's home and shop, as well as the homes of Man'emon's friends and business colleagues, and very quickly uncovered everything that Kinuyo had already told me. In fact they unearthed even more. They also came up with a significant piece of information that would have a great bearing on the case, and almost certainly confirmed Man'emon as the killer.

As I mentioned before, Man'emon was in the process of setting up a new confectionery company. This was to be a limited corporation, without any public offering of shares. The enterprise had been put together by a group of the city's main operators who'd seen their profits eaten away due to pressure from another manufacturer moving into the area. As a way of fighting back they had each procured some capital, and the plan had been to set up a large-scale production facility. Once this was established as a company, Man'emon would take on the role of principal director. A total of 50,000 yen had been raised by the group for the purchase of a factory site and other expenses, and provisionally entrusted to Man'emon, who'd deposited the money in a local bank for the time being. When Saito heard this story from two or three of the store owners, he immediately called on Kinuyo and asked if her husband had any bankbooks in the house. She replied these should all be in the small safe in his study. When this was opened, several bank documents were found, but there was no sign of the book for the 50,000 yen account. When enquiries were made at the bank, it turned out all of the money had been withdrawn in a routine transaction on the morning following the acid murder, shortly after the bank had opened. The bank clerk who dealt with this transaction did not know Man'emon well, and so couldn't say for certain this was the man who had come to withdraw the money. However, all indications were that Man'emon had only made it look like he caught the 4.40 a.m. train to Tokyo that morning, but had in fact stayed in Nagoya waiting for the bank to open. If this was the case, there could hardly be any room for doubt he was the killer.

Even if a murder is committed in the heat of the moment, the terrifying vision of the scaffold soon appears before the eyes of the culprit. It is a simple fact of human nature that Man'emon should then make up his mind to try and escape. And in the case of going on the run, the first thing you need is money. With enough money, you can use every means possible in your attempts to slip through the net of those searching for you. Why had Man'emon returned home as if nothing had happened after committing this atrocious crime? Perhaps to bid farewell one last time to his wife? Or perhaps he came back for a more practical reason – to collect the bankbook for the 50,000 yen account from the safe in his study.

There was one more strange occurrence, unknown to the prosecutor's office or investigating team, that was revealed to me alone. It was something my wife heard directly from Kinuyo. The evening before he was to go to Tokyo, that is the night the body was discovered at the derelict house, just before going to bed, Man'emon behaved in an extraordinary way towards his wife. Acting with deep regret, as though they were to part forever, he displayed an affection he had not shown in years, and then when it seemed like he was about to burst out laughing, tears started to stream down his face and he sobbed wretchedly. As I said previously, the way Man'emon expressed his love towards his wife was very different to what is considered normal, so Kinuyo at first paid no heed to this behaviour, considering it just part of his usual sickness. But then she confided to my wife that thinking on it later, these tears must have had a much deeper significance. She felt acutely that perhaps her husband really was biding a final farewell.

In this way, an unshakable case was built against Man'emon. But it seemed the most concrete evidence of his guilt was that ten days after the crime had been committed there was still no trace of him. Of course a description had been circulated to police stations nationwide, and requests put in for a rigorous manhunt, but Man'emon had simply vanished. The only conclusion was that he was hiding deliberately, doing everything in his power to remain out of sight. At least Akaike, the oddball art student, could finally be released. At the outset of this case it seemed this young man would play a key role, but in the end he was just a rather unfortunate bit player. Soon after his release the poor man's mind went completely, and he was apparently shut away in a lunatic asylum.

And so it came to be, that these two famous emporiums that had sold Nagoya's speciality *Mujina* rice cakes since the Edo era, both met a sorry end, their fates intertwined. But it was Kinuyo who I felt most sympathy for. With her husband gone, her relatives gathered to assess the state of the assets left behind, and it then became clear why Man'emon had fretted so much over the plan to set up a new company. Although he had put on an ostentatious front, in reality the Tanimura family was deep in debt, and Kinuyo had been left with hardly a penny to her name. The venerable old store on T street had been mortgaged as many as three times, and the Tanimura house and its land had been used as security on all the loans. Finally, Kinuyo, possessing only a chest of drawers and a dozen or so outfits, was forced to return in tears to her parent's home, now entirely dependent on them.

It seemed then that the "Case of the Acid Murderer" was now closed. Even I too was convinced of the matter. However, this was not the end of the story. It became apparent that in fact an elaborate and exceedingly bizarre deception had been played, of the kind found in certain novels, and it was the evidence of a set of fingerprints that eventually revealed the truth. Just one single print turned the whole case on its head, and uncovered the real culprit's masterful trickery beyond any doubt. And here I must take some credit myself, as I discovered that print, an act for which I was commended by the prefecture's head of police. Not bad for a rookie detective, don't you think?

This all happened around three weeks after the murder. One day I called on Kinuyo - it had finally been decided that she was to leave her home, and the housemaids were under instructions to pack everything away. While helping with this process I happened to be in my friend's former study when I came across what was clearly Man'emon's old diary. I started scanning through the entries - beginning from the last page – all the time still stuck with the compelling notion that wherever Man'emon was now hiding, he must have been in a torment of regret, wishing he could take back what he had done. The diary itself contained nothing unusual - here and there were several entries cursing over and over Kotono's obstinate behaviour – then I came across a page that caught my eye. In its white margin was the unmistakable mark of a thumbprint. While writing in his diary Man'emon must have got ink on his thumb and then without realizing it, left this impression when turning the page. At first I glanced at this casually, but then with a start, I began to stare intently, as though a hole had opened up and was drawing me in. My complexion must have turned pale, and my breathing ragged, as Kinuyo called out to me when she noticed the look on my face.

"Kinuyo, th...this.." I stammered pointing at the page, "this thumbprint left here, could it be that of your husband's?" I finally asked, as though cross-examining her.

"Yes, certainly. My husband would not let anyone else touch his diary. It must be his without a doubt."

"Then, I wonder, are there any other items only he would have used that might also have his fingerprints left on them? Some lacquerware or silver for instance?"

"There is this silver cigarette case. I can't recall any other such object."

Kinuyo looked startled as I quickly took the cigarette case from her and began to examine it. The outside was spotless, as though it had been polished recently, but when I opened the lid and looked inside, there, as clear as day, on the smooth interior silver surface, mixed in with several other fingerprints, was a perfect match of the diary's thumbprint. One I had recognised immediately.

I'm sure you are thinking it unlikely I could identify a man's fingerprint with just my naked eye, but for professionals like us it is possible with close inspection to compare each prints' pattern of ridges without the aid of a microscope. Even so, just to make sure I took out a magnifying glass from the study's desk drawer and made a more thorough examination, but this only confirmed my initial conclusion.

"Kinuyo, I believe I have made a significant discovery. Please, take a seat, and think carefully before answering my questions."

In my excitement my eyes must have flashed, and I perhaps acted a little forcefully. This fervour must have communicated itself to Kinuyo, as her face went white as she nervously sat down before me.

"Now, first of all, on that evening, the evening before your husband disappeared, I presume Man'emon would have had dinner at home. Could you tell me, in as much detail as possible, exactly what took place?"

This question no doubt came as a complete surprise to Kinuyo, who stared at me unblinking and replied: "Even if I tell you everything, there's nothing much to say really."

That day, Man'emon had retired to his study engrossed in his work. Kinuyo had carried in his dinner and left it beside him, closing the sliding door behind her as she returned to the dining room. After a while, when she judged he had finished, she went back to collect the tray. There was nothing more to add than this it seemed. It was Man'emon's habit – when he was absorbed in some business, or in his writing, or immersed in a book - to shut himself up in his study from morn till night, keeping the staff away, needing only a small charcoal burner next to his desk with an iron kettle so he could make himself tea. He had an ascetic, fastidious streak, like that of an artist.

"And at that time, how did your husband appear? Did he speak to you of anything?"

"No, he said nothing, and I said nothing to him. When he was in this kind of mood he would be sure to fly into a rage if I tried to make conversation, so I left him alone. He was simply hunched over his desk, fixated on his work, and didn't turn to look at me."

"Aha, I see...and then later that evening - this is a little delicate so please forgive me for asking, it is after all a serious matter - I believe your husband finally came to bed after staying in his study until one o'clock. Could you tell me what took place at that time?"

Kinuyo turned a little red around her eyes. She was the kind of woman who blushed easily, which made her seem all the more beautiful. Her radiance even now is burned deep into my memory. Although uncomfortable and turning crimson with embarrassment, Kinuyo felt compelled to answer, as my question was deadly serious.

"We sleep in a room at the back of the house, around eight tatami mats in size. That evening it was late so I retired first, and then, just when I was drifting off, it would have been one o'clock, my husband came to me..."

"Was the room light on at that time?"

"No, it is always my habit to turn off the bedroom light. However the light in the hall was still on and shone through the screen door, so it was not completely dark."

"And did your husband speak to you then? Please, I assure you I don't wish to ask about anything else that might have happened, if you could only tell me whether there was any general conversation that evening in your bedroom between you and Man'emon? Or something connected to the household?"

"No, nothing of that sort...as far as I remember we didn't have such a conversation."

"And then he was awake again before four o'clock. What took place at that time?"

"I overslept and didn't notice my husband get up. That morning it happened there was a problem with the electricity, and when I woke I saw by candlelight that my husband was already dressed. He must have changed in the dressing room while I was still asleep. Then a rickshaw arrived that had been ordered the night before, so I and one of the maids, carrying candles of course, went to the front entrance to see my husband off."

Now, I am giving you only a shortened version of all this so you may grasp the main points. If I repeated everything that passed between myself and Kinuyo that day I'm sure I would only bore you. This is why the conversation sounds a little stilted and unrealistic. Of course if I'd really been as blunt as this I would not have been able to draw out the information I'd been looking for. In truth my questioning of Kinuyo went on for more than an hour.

"So in short, that morning Man'emon left without taking any breakfast? Reasonable enough I suppose, considering the hour, and the fact it would still have been dark at that time of year."

In this way I thoroughly quizzed Kinuyo, asking her everything I felt was relevant. And all the while as I continued this apparently arbitrary questioning, my heart thumped in my chest and my palms began to sweat. The fantastical notion that had formed in my mind at that moment still felt too preposterous to be true – an outrageous long shot - but the more I heard about what took place that evening, the more my strange fancy seemed to take on the solid contours of reality.

"So from that evening till the next morning, would it be true to say you never once had a clear look at your husband's countenance? And furthermore you never engaged in any significant conversation?" When I put this last question to Kinuyo, for a while she was silent, unable to grasp the reasoning behind my words. Then little by little her expression changed, until finally it became one of pure horror, as though she had just encountered some awful spectre.

"Please, what is it you are trying to say? What is the meaning of all these questions?"

"The fact of the matter is, how confident can you be that that person really was your husband?"

"But, surely there's no way...it's impossible."

"You never saw his face clearly. And why, just for that evening, was he so taciturn? Please think carefully, was it normal for your husband to pass a whole night without spending any time in conversation? Leaving aside him shutting himself up in his study, there must have been some instructions he would have wished to leave before going away?"

"It is true, he was remarkably silent. He was never usually so quiet before going on a trip. But please, I feel as though I may lose all sense, don't delay any more, I beg you, what is it you really think happened?"

I'm sure you can well imagine Kinuyo's shock and horror in that moment. I myself naturally could not pry any further, and of course Kinuyo would not touch on so delicate a matter, for it would have been the greatest disgrace to her as a woman if the man in her bedroom that night had not been Man'emon. As I said earlier, according to what I heard from my wife, Man'emon had acted in a way most unlike his usual self. On the point of laughter, he had suddenly wept, his hot tears soaking Kinuyo's own soft cheeks. It had seemed a certainty those tears were down to Man'emon's turbulent state of mind at committing a murder, and he had wept so wretchedly for he knew he would be leaving his wife forever. But if that person was not Man'emon, then the longing embrace, the laughter, and the tears held an altogether more loathsome significance.

You may well wonder how such an absurd feat could be possible. But then, have there not been cases in the past where those of a superior criminal mind have pulled off apparently impossible acts quite easily? And have their notorious deeds not been written into criminal history bringing them immortal fame?

As for Kinuyo, there are no words to describe such misfortune. Although she had failed to notice what was right in front of her, she had committed no crime. The imposter's plan was so deviant, so outside the normal bounds of reason.

In the same way that all material objects are governed by the peculiar force of inertia, human psychology also works according to its own momentum. Kinuyo had believed the man sitting in her husband's study, working at her husband's desk, wearing her husband's kimono, whose figure from behind appeared exactly like that of her husband, was without any doubt her husband. And as long as some turn of events did not change this, would remain so (although later, unbeknownst to Kinuyo, it became clear events had changed). It is also natural she would believe it was her husband who later emerged from his study, and that this misapprehension would continue in their bedroom, and until he departed the next morning.

At the same time, the imposter had to be extremely cautious for such an audacious act to work - and in this case perform the subtle trick of an electrical fault to take out the lights. According to Kinuyo, when she later had someone from the electric company come and fix this problem, it turned out there was no fault at all, but that the cover of the main switch box - fitted above the door in the kitchen - had been opened and the power cut. In other words, all the imposter had to do was creep into the kitchen while everyone was asleep and remove this cover. It's clear he had carefully calculated that in the hustle and bustle of him leaving the next morning the housemaids would not have noticed such a thing, since in most households no-one pays any attention to this switch.

Finally, on the brink of tears, Kinuyo tentatively asked me: "Well then, if you are saying that person was not my husband, who could it possibly have been?"

"Please do not be alarmed," I replied, "but my supposition - indeed no longer a supposition, I think there can now be hardly any doubt – I believe that person was in fact Shuichi Kotono."

When she heard this, Kinuyo's perfect face crumpled like that of a sobbing child. "No, no, there's no way that can be true. What are you saying? What kind of fantasy is this? Wasn't it Kotono that was killed in that derelict house? And wasn't his murder on that very same evening?" Kinuyo, now clutching at straws, desperately tried to deny the awful truth of the matter.

"I'm afraid it was not. There are no words to express how deeply regrettable this is, but the person killed that night was not

Shuichi Kotono. It was in fact Man'emon Tanimura. Your husband." Finally I had no choice but to utter these words out loud.

Poor Kinuyo. While she had still believed her husband was only missing, hiding in some corner of the world, there had always been the hope they might meet again someday. But now, although she must have felt some relief he was not the murderer - to know it was Man'emon whose skin had been so blistered as to appear like the flesh of a burst pomegranate – to know it was Man'emon who had been killed in such an atrocious manner - her pain must have been overwhelming. On top of this, she now knew the man who had slept in her bed that night had not been her husband. Instead it had been a sworn enemy of the Tanimura family, a person vehemently loathed by Man'emon himself...but, that aside, more than anything, it had been her husband's own killer, the man who had forced sulphuric acid down his throat. As a woman, and as a wife, this must have been too much to bear. Her lips were dry and had lost all colour when she spoke again: "I still can't quite believe this to be true. Is there any positive evidence? Please, do not hold back if you have more to say."

"There is, I'm afraid, conclusive evidence. As you yourself have confirmed, the fingerprints on this diary and this cigarette box belong to your husband. These prints are also a perfect match of those taken off the body in the derelict house in town G."

Now, at that time there was not yet a fingerprint index for the prefecture, but since in this case the victim was so horribly disfigured, and there was no other easy means of identification, as a precaution, fingerprints had been taken from the body so they could at least be checked against criminal records held in Tokyo. As a keen young officer and lover of detective stories I had a special interest in the science of fingerprinting, and went so far as to carefully classify this set according to the Hamburg method. And although of course it was not possible for me to remember the exact shape of every particular ridge, there was a distinctive detail about the victim's right thumbprint that was easy to recall. This print had an "ulnar loop" pattern - that is to say it was hoof shaped, with its two ends pointing towards the little finger – and had exactly seven ridges from its outer to inner edge. This gave it a value of 3 according to the classification system. There was nothing particularly memorable about this except that cutting across this loop in a diagonal direction was a small scar. Two prints with the same pattern, the same number of ridges and the same scar was almost unthinkable. This then was irrefutable proof that the body in that derelict house belonged not to Shuichi Kotono, but to Man'emon Tanimura. Of course I later made a careful comparison of the thumbprint in the diary with the records we had of the victim's prints back at the station, and confirmed there could be no mistake, the two were identical in every way.

Needless to say I reported all the details of this startling discovery and what it meant for the case to my superior officer. It also goes without saying that everyone at the station – indeed all the regional press - were left utterly astounded when their assumptions about the guilty party in this crime were completely overturned by one set of prints. As I was still young and foolish, I myself couldn't help feeling a little jubilant at all the fuss.

You may well laugh at our stupidity in not spotting this earlier. How could we miss a device so common to detective stories? Did we not find it suspicious acid had been used to keep the body from being identified? Why were we so eager to accept the victim was Kotono? Well, we did briefly have our suspicions, both in the public prosecutor's office and at the station. But in this case a truly bold and cunning sleight of hand had been played – one that dispelled all doubts, even made us forget we had such doubts in the first place. At the heart of this crime was a virtuoso performance in Man'emon's study and bedroom that had even ensnared the victim's wife – one that made us all believe Man'emon was still alive, at least until the following morning, and could not possibly have been killed that night.

Hearing Kinuyo's testimony, it had been reasonable to assume Man'emon and Kotono had met that evening. And if we were made to think Man'emon had survived that meeting, then considering everything that happened before and after the murder, the only possible conclusion we could come to was that Kotono was the victim. Both men were of the same build, and both had their hair cropped short, so it was naturally hard to tell them apart if their clothes were changed and one of their faces disfigured. Also if it was assumed Man'emon was still alive, there would have been no danger of Kinuyo visiting the scene and inspecting the body – which would have been the murderer's greatest fear. Everything had been cleverly thought through from beginning to end it seemed. But, as so often in detective novels, the murderer had made one mistake. Although they had gone to the trouble of destroying the victim's face, they had neglected to destroy an even more effective means of identification, the victim's fingerprints. In the parlance of such stories, this was the blunder that confirmed Kotono's guilt.

Even so, what a brilliantly conceived crime it was. In one stroke Kotono had dispatched in the cruellest manner his ancestors' mortal enemy – indeed conveniently for Kotono it was the cruelty of the method that meant he was to evade suspicion – while at the same time, if only for one night, he could play husband and wife with the woman he had for so many years longed for – which also served a crucial role in covering up evidence of his guilt. Furthermore, by stealing the bank book from the safe in the study, he was immediately transformed from miserable penury to great wealth. In simple terms, he had killed three birds with one stone. This was the kind of magic trick usually performed by fairy tale conjurors.

Thinking about it later, Kotono's custom of shamelessly calling on the Tanimura's residence before the murder - acting as though he no longer held any grudge - was not simply so he could gaze upon Kinuyo's face. In fact his motive must have been to learn everything he could about the married couple's habits, the layout of the house, how to open the safe in the study, the whereabouts of Man'emon's legally registered seal, and the location of the main electricity switch. He must have waited until the bank book for the new company's investment fund could be found in that safe, and then chosen an evening which came before Man'emon had planned a trip to Tokyo. He must have put a great deal of thought into his scheme.

As is the way of all fictional detectives let me finally describe Kotono's movements on the night of the murder, though it may be unnecessary by now. First of all he made ready a bottle of sulphuric acid then lay in wait at the derelict house; when Man'emon entered he quickly overpowered him, tied his hands and feet and then mercilessly killed him; he then untied the ropes, swapped clothes with his victim, and once again tied him up; Kotono, now in the guise of Man'emon, hid the empty bottle, then taking extra care not to be stopped by anyone on the way, entered the Tanimura's residence by the back gate and shut himself away in the study. From this point, I have already described in detail the order of events, so there is no need to say any more.

And so, once and for all, the "Case of the Acid Murderer" was solved.

5

At length, I apologized to Inomata for taking up so much of his time: "I hope you weren't inconvenienced too much - but I am grateful - in relating this tale I have now vividly recalled all that took place back then. I must now try and record it in my journal as soon as possible."

"Inconvenience me? Not a bit of it", he replied, "it was most fascinating. Not only are you a renowned detective but also a magnificent storyteller. I haven't spent such a pleasant time in years," Inomata went on, curiously showering me with praise. He then added, "there is one thing I'd like to ask however, although your story made perfect sense, you never mentioned whether the true culprit, Kotono, was ever captured or not?"

"I'm afraid to say he was never apprehended," I answered. "His photograph was reproduced in large quantities and distributed to the main police stations around the country, as well as his description, but it seems if one person really decides to disappear, then disappear they can. It's nearly ten years past, so there's little chance of him turning up now. He must be somewhere out of sight of the law, or perhaps no longer living. Even if he were alive, the case is mostly forgotten - I was directly involved and yet it had slipped my mind too - so I can't see him ever being brought to justice."

At this Inomata grinned and stared straight at me. "So it's true to say you never got a confession from the murderer himself. You only have the exemplary reasoning of such an accomplished detective as yourself."

There seemed to be a touch of sarcasm in Inomata's words. I felt strangely uncomfortable and remained silent. Troubled by something, Inomata stared vacantly at the blackness beneath us. It was almost dusk and the leaden sky was becoming increasingly dark. It felt as if all of creation was being smothered by this dull light. The mountains in the distance were almost completely black, and something like a thin, hazy mist had settled on the dark pool below. Nothing moved as far as the eye could see, it was as though we were in a dead world. The far off rumbling of the waterfall now had an ominous quality that seemed to match the beat and rhythm of my own mood.

Finally, Inomata lifted his gaze from the abyss and threw me a significant look. The coloured lenses in his glasses caught the dim light and flashed for a moment. Through them I could see his large double lidded eyes. From early on I had noticed that his left eye never seemed to blink - meaning it had to be false. It appeared he did not wear tinted glasses because his sight was poor, but to hide the fact he had a glass eye. For no particular reason I considered this as I returned his gaze, when he suddenly began to speak again, changing the subject completely.

"You are aware I am sure of the children's game 'Rock, Paper, Scissors'? I happen to be rather good, perhaps you'd like to play? Though I don't think you'd be much of a match for me."

I was taken aback for a moment and said nothing, but then feeling irritated by his childish challenge agreed to play and held out my right hand. For a while our gruff adult voices echoed across the silent gorge repeating "One, two, three, go! One, two, three, go!". It turned out Inomata really was very good at the game. At first we were fairly evenly matched, but then he grew overwhelmingly stronger, and no matter how much it vexed me I simply couldn't beat him. In the end I had to admit defeat, and laughing, Inomata explained himself: "Well, what do you make of that eh? You see, 'Rock, Paper, Scissors' is not such child's play. The game has hidden depths - I dare say its principles are even a question of mathematical psychology. For instance, let's say you begin with 'Paper' and are beaten by 'Scissors'. A naive child might immediately decide next time to play 'Rock' which wins against 'Scissors'. This method is the most infantile. A more cunning child might assume their opponent will anticipate this with 'Paper', and therefore they themselves should play 'Scissors'. This level of calculation is about the average. However, an even more cunning child's approach might be this: I first lost with 'Paper', so the assumption is I will play 'Rock' next. My opponent will anticipate this and choose 'Paper', therefore the obvious thing is to play 'Scissors'. However, my opponent should also have anticipated this, and will actually play 'Rock'. To counteract this, the winning move in the end should be 'Paper'. In this way, by always staying one step ahead they never lose at the game.

"This kind of approach is not just limited to 'Rock, Paper, Scissors', it can be applied to all aspects of human conflict. The combatant who can strategize at a deeper level than their rival will always be victorious - and the same goes for criminal activity too don't you think? Cops and robbers are constantly involved in this contest of 'Rock, Paper, Scissors'. And it's certainly true that by meticulously studying the thought processes of prosecutors and the police, certain criminal masterminds are always able to act in anticipation of their opponent's next move. Indeed, isn't this how they evade capture for so long?"

Here Inomata stopped for a moment, and once more looked at me and grinned. "You are also aware I'm sure of Edgar Allan

Poe's 'The Purloined Letter'? There is a young boy in this story said to be very intelligent, and brilliant at the guessing game of 'Odds and Evens' – using a slightly different method to the one I just outlined. When asked what his secret was, the boy explained: 'If I want to know how smart or ignorant my opponent is, whether they are a good or bad person, what they are thinking right at that moment, I try as much as possible to mimic their facial expression. Once I have matched myself to them, I carefully examine the emotion this stirs within me.' Poe's detective Dupin apparently maintained that the boy's answer was more profound than the philosophies of Machiavelli and Tommaso Campanella. I wonder, when you were investigating the 'Case of the Acid Murderer' if you ever thought to imitate the expressions of your supposed culprit? I think not perhaps. Indeed, just now when we were playing 'Rock, Paper, Scissors' you seemed completely oblivious to this approach."

Inamoto's long-winded speech and niggling manner were beginning to get on my nerves. What exactly was he trying to say? I couldn't help firing back a sarcastic question of my own: "Listening to you now, it seems that you think my reasoning in this case was at fault somehow, and the culprit was able to outwit me. Perhaps you have some alternative hypothesis to put forward?"

Again Inomata grinned. "I don't think it would be terribly difficult for someone who stays one step ahead to overturn everything you surmised in this case. In exactly the same way the discovery of a single set of fingerprints completely reversed all your previous assumptions, is there not something you missed that could upset your reasoning once again?"

Hearing this I felt my blood rise. How dare he talk to me this way? After my many years of experience as a detective. "Well then, I'd certainly like to hear what you have to say. Please tell me what I missed that turns all my deductions on their head."

"Certainly, as you wish...it's such a trivial thing really, but can you be certain that the fingerprints you found on the diary and cigarette case were not actually a contrivance?"

"A contrivance?"

"Let me put it this way - although these items would normally have had Man'emon's fingerprints on them, it's not hard to imagine someone else's prints could have been deliberately planted instead."

I remained silent. The significance of what Inomata was saying had not yet sunk in, but there was something in his words that made me shudder.

"Perhaps now you are just beginning to understand. It was Man'emon's plan to use his own personal possessions, those items he'd kept closest to him, and arrange to have the prints of another man left on them. If this other person were someone who visited frequently this would not have been such a difficult task. You only paid attention to the diary and cigarette case, but I'm sure if you searched longer, the same prints would have been found on other similar objects."

"What you say is possible I suppose. But what 'other person' are you talking about?"

"Why Kotono of course", Inomata replied without any change in his voice. "For a time Kotono often dropped in at the house, did he not? It would have been easy for Man'emon to have Kotono leave his fingerprints without arousing any suspicion. And it goes without saying at the same time he would have carefully wiped away every one of his own prints from those places where someone might expect to find them."

"So they were Kotono's fingerprints?...But that makes no sense." It's embarrassing now to think of my slow-witted response, but at that moment I was falling into a kind of stupor.

"It makes perfect sense...I'm afraid you are still labouring under a misapprehension - your belief that Man'emon was killed in that derelict house – and this is clouding your judgement. Let's say it wasn't Man'emon, but as you first surmised Kotono instead, then the fingerprints you took off the body would of course be Kotono's. And if the prints deliberately left on the diary were also Kotono's, then naturally these two sets would match."

"And the murderer?" Now under Inomata's spell, all I could do was keep repeating foolish questions.

"Is without doubt the person who had arranged to have Kotono's prints left there: Man'emon Tanimura." Inomata loftily asserted this apparently irrefutable fact with such conviction it was as though he had witnessed the crime himself. "You yourself knew Man'emon was beset by money problems. His shop was doomed to bankruptcy; he had debts of hundreds of thousands of yen which could only be settled by the sale of his estate. Rather than endure this humiliation, how much better to flee with 50,000 in cash. Even so, as the only motive for his actions this is still a little tenuous - Man'emon had not killed Kotono by chance, he had planned it long before and bided his time. So what reason other than money could he have had? And how could he have been so indifferent to the torment he would put Kinuyo through? The only possible answer is another woman. You see, Man'emon was in love - and what's more, with another man's wife. Sooner or later these two lovebirds were destined to fly away together, far from the world's gaze. Finally, as a third motive, there was of course the long-standing grudge Man'emon held towards his victim. Love, money, and hate. To borrow your own words, his plan effectively killed three birds with one stone.

"At that time you were well acquainted with Man'emon, and he knew that as an avid fan of detective novels - unlike more practical thinking officers - you possessed a rather fanciful temperament. Without you he could not have come up with such an elaborate plan - in short, he singled you out as his target - you were the basis for his whole scheme. Just like the young boy who played 'Odds and Evens', he mimicked your facial expressions; just like in 'Rock, Paper, Scissors', he stayed one step ahead; and you played right into his hands. A masterful criminal needs an exceptional detective as their adversary. It is because you were his that he could pull off such a trick.

"For Man'emon, his twisted plan also had an attraction beyond the grasp of ordinary men. As you know...no, perhaps far more than you imagined, Man'emon was a true disciple of the notorious Marquis de Sade. He'd tired of Kinuyo, but his final performance for her was something really marvellous. Man'emon took on the role of Kotono, playing Man'emon himself. Careful not to speak or show his face, for a short time he fully became the part. And in an act so outlandish - unable to contain his laughter, perhaps, or his tears - he illicitly consummated the love of another man for his own wife.

"Also, as you will realize, Man'emon's savage actions had another purpose. Displaying the creative power of his own sadism he utilized the cruellest of all murder methods. A little while ago you described the victim's face as being like a 'burst pomegranate'. Yes, a 'burst pomegranate' - Man'emon was seduced by this terrible notion - it became his starting point, so to speak. What reason could there be to kill a man and then turn their face into an unrecognizable mess of wounds? Of course the investigating officer only needed a little acumen to guess a deception had been played. With the victim dressed in Kotono's clothes they would eventually be led to believe it was not actually Kotono but only made to look that way, and another man had to be the victim. However, this was exactly what Man'emon wanted. In reality Kotono had been killed, as it first had seemed.

"Accordingly, the bottle of sulphuric acid had not been brought to the house by Kotono, but purchased by Man'emon, who placed it there in preparation. After he had finished his work that night he disposed of the empty bottle in a roadside gutter on his way home. Then came his performance. Man'emon - in the guise of Kotono posing as Man'emon - nervously crept into his own study as though he were breaking into a stranger's house."

Inomata's assertions left me utterly astonished. Who was this man? How had he come up with such a wild theory? He was too insistent and employing too much detail for this to be mere playful speculation. Since I remained silent, Inomata began to speak again: "Some time ago, I had a friend who was also a lover of detective fiction. He often came to my house and we would share our observations on criminality. On one occasion we were speculating on the most ingenious trick a murderer could play.

We concluded this to be the double-cross, where the culprit made themselves appear the victim. Although a rather novel idea, when we tried to think of actual examples all we came up with were well worn ploys such as someone with an incurable illness making their suicide look like murder to set someone else up for the crime; or if several people were killed, the murderer could hide amongst his victims - apparently being the only one to survive the attack - wounding himself to avoid suspicion. I felt strongly however that these lacked cunning, and there had to be a more devious device available to the more exceptionally minded criminal. My friend insisted that since we had failed to think of one ourselves such a trick did not exist, and this turned into quite an argument between us. But just now, have I not been proved right? In other words, although for many years it was accepted that Man'emon was the victim in the 'Case of the Acid Murderer', if my reasoning is correct, the real culprit had actually performed such a double-cross, and Man'emon was in fact the killer.

"The trick you were convinced had taken place seemed clever enough. But for one man to take on the guise of another man, and spend a whole evening with that other man's wife - is such a stunt really possible? The notion is perhaps stranger than fiction, which is exactly why you and others were so seduced by it."

As Inomata spoke, some dim and faraway recollection seemed to stir within me. Somehow I felt we had talked like this before, but I had only met Inomata a few days ago, he could not have been the figure in my memory. So who was I thinking of? I had the sensation I was looking at a ghost - that something large and undefined was right before my eyes, dreadful and indeterminate - but try as I might I could not grasp its true form.

In that moment Inomata's behaviour took an even more bizarre turn. He stopped speaking and stared straight at me. Then flashing me a curious look suddenly put both hands to his jaw and with a jerky movement extracted a set of upper and lower dentures. His mouth became like that of a toothless 80-year-old woman. Without the support of those false teeth the space below his nose had now compressed, and his whole face was squashed flat like a Chinese lantern.

As I mentioned at the beginning of my story, Inomata had a rather appealing appearance. Although completely bald, this gave him an intellectual air. His Roman nose and sharply trimmed beard added to the effect. But by removing his dentures the spell had been broken. He suddenly looked so wretched it made me marvel at how much a person's features can be transformed. His wrinkled face was now that of an old crone, or a new born baby. Inomata took off his tinted glasses and screwed up both his eyes. While his lips smacked together feebly, he started to speak again, his words now hard to make out: "Look carefully at me. Now picture my eyes with single lids. And my eyebrows thick and bushy. Next, imagine my nose was a little flatter, and my bald head, instead of being smooth, was covered with hair, cropped short...Well? Now do you understand? Search your memory, is this face not familiar to you?"

Inomata thrust his face forward for my inspection, keeping his eyes tightly shut. I did as I'd been told and imagined his appearance with the changes he'd described. Then, just like a picture suddenly coming into focus, a truly unexpected figure popped into my mind. Now everything made sense, and I finally understood why Inomata had been able to speak so authoritatively just now. I couldn't stop myself from exclaiming loudly: "I've got it! It's you, Man'emon Tanimura!"

"That's right old friend. I am indeed. It took a little time for the penny to drop didn't it? That's most unlike you," Inomata, or rather Man'emon, chuckled softly to himself, then continued, "although you are probably still asking yourself how is it possible I have changed so much."

Man'emon then placed his dentures back in his mouth so he could continue with his story more clearly: "I'm sure way back then we once discussed the possibilities of disguise. Well, I simply put my own theory into practice. After going to the bank and withdrawing that 50,000 yen, I made some small changes to my appearance and fled straight away to Shanghai - along with my mistress, who was indeed a married woman. As you yourself mentioned it was two whole days before the body in that derelict house was identified as Kotono, so I didn't feel in any immediate danger. By the time I came under suspicion we had already made it to Korea, and were enduring a long and tedious train journey. I was fearful of a sea voyage. For criminals on the run, boarding a steamship can feel like being locked in a cage. In Shanghai we rented some rooms and stayed there for a year. I'd rather not go too deeply into my emotions at the time, but let me just say it was a very happy twelve months. Kinuyo was by any normal standards a beautiful woman, but she was a poor match for me. I preferred the gloomy, seductress type, a Femme Fatale just like Akiko, the lady I had escaped with. I was utterly besotted with her, and still am even now. If it were only possible to feel differently, but there was nothing I could do.

"While in Shanghai to protect myself against all possibilities I set about a full-scale transformation. In my opinion a proper disguise is not a matter of make-up, false beards, and hairpieces. What I did was to thoroughly and obsessively erase my own existence from this world and create an entirely new person. There are some excellent hospitals in Shanghai, mostly operated by foreigners, and from these I picked out separate specialists in dentistry, ophthalmology, and plastic surgery - choosing ones that most suited my needs - and then I doggedly pursued my goal. My first thought was to lose my thicker than normal hair. Growing hair back is a rather difficult proposition - but not so for removing it - all that's necessary is some hair removal lotion. At the same time I had my eyebrows thinned in the same way. Next came my nose. As you will remember my nose used to be rather flat and unattractive. However using ivory implants I was able to give it a more noble, Roman appearance. After this I decided to alter the outline of my face. This was actually easier than you imagine, all I needed was to have some dentures made. My lower jaw used to protrude slightly outwards, and I suffered terribly from tooth decay, so I decided to have all my teeth removed and as my gums were quite thin, have some thicker dentures fitted which were able to produce an over-bite effect, completely reversing how my jawline looked previously. In this way my features, as you see them now, were utterly transformed. Indeed you only recognised my true identity once those dentures were removed. After this, as you can see I grew a beard, and all that was left were my eyes. You know, when it comes to disguising oneself the eyes are the most troublesome area. First of all I had surgery to alter my eyelids from single to double lidded. This was fairly straightforward, but somehow I wasn't satisfied. I thought about feigning some persistent optical disorder which meant I had to wear dark glasses all the time, but this seemed too easy. 'Was there a better way?' I wondered. Finally, I made up my mind to sacrifice one of my eyes. In other words deliberately replace one with a glass replica. I could then use this as an excuse for having tinted lenses - people would assume I was simply trying to hide my ocular prosthesis – and the eye itself would bring a great change in my appearance...well, there you have it. In this way every aspect of my face became an artificial construction. I had erased all trace of Man'emon Tanimura from my features. Although Akiko often teased me that my countenance still held lingering evidence of its original beauty..."

Man'emon told his extraordinary tale as though it were the most natural thing in the world, and as he spoke, he reached up with his right hand and scooped out the false eye from his left socket and showed it to me. It appeared like an upturned glass bowl, and while toying with it between his fingers he turned to me again - his sunken empty socket now a black hole in his face - and continued: "Once I had been completely transformed we returned together to Japan. Shanghai is a wonderful city, but as Japanese citizens we couldn't forget our homeland. We flitted around various hot spring resorts, living like travellers from another world - for nearly ten years it was as though we were the only two people on the earth."

The one-eyed Man'emon looked out sadly across the deep gorge. "It's strange isn't it? For you to recall the 'Case of the Acid

Murderer' today of all days, I'd never dreamed such a thing...perhaps, it was always meant to be."

Suddenly this occurred to me too. If this was a coincidence, what a truly horrifying one - but then Man'emon began to laugh softly to himself: "You still haven't caught on have you? No, this was no accident of fate. In fact I made sure you told that story. Remember the book? The one we talked about on the way to coming here? That was part of my plan. You said earlier that you couldn't recall the plot to 'Trent's Last Case' by E. C. Bentley, but you had not completely forgotten, in the back of your mind something remained. In that story a murder takes place, and the killer disguises himself as his victim. His trick is to then enter the murdered man's study and deceive that man's own wife. Isn't this identical to your solution to the 'Case of the Acid Murderer'? When you saw that book's title you unconsciously made this association. Now look closer, doe this copy not look familiar to you? See how someone has written their impressions on the page in red pencil. Don't you recognise the handwriting?"

I brought the book closer and inspected the notes written in red - instantly their significance dawned on me. It was all so long ago it had completely slipped my mind. Back then I was still a lowly paid junior officer and could not afford to buy detective novels myself, so I would visit Man'emon and borrow new editions from him. 'Trent's Last Case' was one of these. I remembered now that after reading it I wrote down some of my thoughts in the margin. In other words, that handwriting in red pencil was my own.

Man'emon seemed to have said all he wanted, and was now silent. I too did not speak for a while. I was turning round and round in my mind one final puzzle. What on earth was the meaning behind this reunion Man'emon had engineered? What hidden motive did he have for confessing to me now, after all the pain and effort he had already gone through to avoid punishment? Could it be that he'd made a monumental error? This crime had not yet reached its statute of limitations. Had he miscalculated and believed he was now free from prosecution? Perhaps he was intending to ridicule me should I make any high-handed attempts to arrest him. In the end I asked directly: "But why are you telling me all of this? Do you imagine the time limit has passed on this crime and the law has no hold over you?"

But Man'emon's expression did not change. Slowly he responded: "No, I would not consider anything so cowardly. I don't even know clearly when that limit would be...the reason why I confessed to you now is down to my own sadistic nature. You see, I defeated you. You fell for my trap entirely. But you never knew this - instead you preened over your own brilliant deduction. This always ate away at my soul. I wanted you to know, I wanted to say to you 'Well, are you beaten now?'"

So this was why Man'emon had acted so maliciously, getting me to make a fool of myself before revealing the truth. But what now? Was I really just going to admit defeat and leave it at that?

"Certainly I've been beaten. There's nothing more I can say on that point. But even so, I am still a police officer, and as such I have no choice but to arrest you. It must be very gratifying to have got the better of me, but on the other hand you have gifted me an even greater prize, the capture of such a merciless killer as yourself." While saying this I grabbed Man'emon's wrist but with incredible force he immediately broke free.

"Now, now, that won't do. Remember how back in the old days we often tested each other's strength? Didn't I always come out on top? You know you can't overpower me - why do you think I chose such a lonely spot as this? All part of my plan of course. If you tried to arrest me I would only have to give a little push and down into the gorge you would go - Ha! But do not fear, I am only playing, it is not my intention to escape. Indeed, you can watch me end this matter myself – and you won't have to lift a finger...you see, there is nothing I desire from this world anymore. Any attachment I held has gone. The one reason I had for living, Akiko, died just one month ago, from acute pneumonia. And I made her a promise on her deathbed that I would soon follow her into the gates of hell - after I had completed one final task, to meet with you and tell you everything. And so, now that is done, I bid you farewell..."

The last syllable of Man'emon's "farewell" seemed to drop towards the bottom of the gorge like a falling arrow. Catching me unawares, he had leapt head first into the black pool far below.

I immediately leant forward and stared down into the darkness, my breath rasping and my heart pounding in my ears. I caught sight of something white, decreasing in size, that seemed to disrupt the surface of the water with a splash - then as soon as the pool had settled for a second, several large rings began to expand outwards in waves. A moment later in the centre of those rings, there seemed to my delirious eyes a giant smashed pomegranate, its crimson flesh burst open.

After a while the pool became still once more. The early evening mist began to wrap itself around the mountains and the valley - nothing else stirred - the noise of the waterfall continued its eternal rhythm, eventually harmonizing with my own heartbeat. When finally I drew myself up from my position overlooking the gorge, brushing away the sand from my kimono, my eye happened to fall on a memento Man'emon had left behind on the dry white surface of the rock. His glass eye, small and serene on top of the dark cover of E. C. Bentley's detective novel. That pearl-like eye seemed to be murmuring some mysterious fable to itself, as it gazed up at the leaden sky.

The Devouring Insects

(虫)

The story of Masaki Aizou and Fuyuo Kinoshita really begins the night they had their fateful reunion, but before I come to that, I must first give an account of our protagonist's remarkable personality.

Masaki Aizou was an only child. At the time this story takes place both his parents were no longer living and he had inherited a reasonably sized estate. He was 27, unmarried, had given up his studies and did not work. In short he had the leisurely carefree life the envy of every street beggar or family man. However he could not enjoy his position as he happened to suffer from a severe kind of misanthropy.

Why he was inflicted with this abnormal trait he himself did not know, but the signs were there early in his childhood. As a young boy, his eyes would well up should another person simply look at him. He would awkwardly stare at the ceiling or use his hands to conceal his tears but the more he tried to hide his embarrassment the more self-conscious he became; even more tears would flow until he would finally cry out in complete panic. He acted this way towards his father, the servants, even his mother, so naturally began to avoid the company of others. Although he longed for human contact he had to withdraw from it, as he feared his own shameful nature. His only comfort was found in those times he would hide away in a dark corner of the front parlour, constructing elaborate castle walls from wooden building blocks, mumbling improvised nursery rhymes to himself.

As he grew older he was forced to enter the alarming world of education, and being such a peculiar child one can only wonder at the bewilderment and terror he must have felt. He found the shame of his mother knowing of his condition hard to bear, so he would keep his school life secret from her. While there, his social interactions were really quite pathetic. If one of his teachers or classmates said anything to him at all, tears would form in his eyes and there was nothing he could do to stop them. He'd cry simply at overhearing his name being mentioned by his form tutor when talking with a colleague.

During high school and university this detestable shyness gradually lessened, but at elementary school he missed a third of the year through sickness and convalescence. At middle school he feigned illness for half the year, skipping classes and shutting himself up in his study. He would order the servants to stay away and spend his time reading novels or lost in absurd daydreams. At university he hardly set foot inside the classroom (other than for taking exams), although not because he was out enjoying the company of his fellow students, instead he would bury himself under the mountain of eccentric books he had amassed. But rather than read these moldy old poetic texts and English 18th century leather bound volumes, he would smell their pages and immerse himself in the mysterious vapor that seemed to emanate from them, falling deeper and deeper into fantasy, completely unaware if it was day or night outside.

Since he was such a strange fellow he had no friends to speak of - apart from one, who I will come to later - and certainly no lovers. And yet he was unusually sensitive, and longed for companionship and affection. When he heard or read stories of intimate friendships and romances he always wondered at how happy these would make him - and envied those who'd had such experiences - but even if he harbored such feelings he could never express them. There was something blocking him like a wall standing in his path.

Masaki viewed all of humanity as mean spirited, with himself being the only exception. He knew if he ever confided in anyone they would only betray him. When he was in middle school he often marveled at the people he saw talking together on the train. While one spoke enthusiastically the other would listen with a blank expression on their face, turning to look out of the window - occasionally they might nod in agreement as though something had occurred to them, but mostly they hardly glanced at the speaker - then when the opportunity arose they would suddenly take up the conversation while their partner would now be the one to turn away indifferently. It took many years for Masaki to understand this was the usual way for people to converse. Although most people would find this kind of thing trivial, such examples of human behavior were enough to silence the introverted Masaki (he also found jokes in everyday conversation utterly baffling; for him they seemed mostly cheap cracks that were simply unpleasant and entirely malicious in nature). Whenever he spoke, if the person he was talking to looked away for a moment and seemed to lose interest, Masaki's bashfulness caused his words to dry up in his mouth.

He was greedy for love, but because his greed was so great, perhaps love and normal social interaction were beyond him - but this was not all, there was another aspect to Masaki's eccentricity. When he was very young, if he put his bedding away in the morning to help the maids out (to give an everyday example) his mother, who was still alive at the time, would cry, "Oh what a good boy!" and give him a reward. But being praised only embarrassed him; so much so that he felt his whole body become hot. This feeling was so unpleasant he began to hate intensely whoever was giving him praise. And so eventually, while in one respect he ached to love and be loved, at the same time these feelings were loathsome to him in a way that was hard to describe. They gripped his insides and twisted them. Such emotions as had been invested in him could perhaps only be described as self-disgust, and a contempt towards his family and all others. It was totally bewildering to him that people could be so brazenly and casually cheerful despite all the meanness there was. It seemed he was a species of creature separate from the rest of humanity, completely foreign to this world. A solitary beast in the shadows, by some chance abandoned here from another land.

How was it such a person could end up so wildly in love? Well stranger things have happened I suppose. Perhaps it was because of the way he was that he loved with such an unearthly mania - perhaps for him, love and hate were simply one and the same. But I am getting ahead of myself, I will return to this theme later on.

For a short time after his parents died, Masaki kept up appearances for the sake of his relations, but before long he withdrew from society. Without a second thought he dropped out of university, sold the family home and its land, and moved to a rundown, desolate house on the edge of town that he'd had his eye on for some time. In so doing he vanished from the world he'd known. Although it's impossible to completely ignore the rest of the human race, for a while Masaki felt relief at moving somewhere he was a stranger. What he hated most was people knowing his name and everything about him, but here he could escape such prying eyes.

His new residence was in a neighborhood called town K, a little upstream from Azumabashi bridge, in the Mukojima ward of Tokyo. There was a red light district nearby and a dense area of cheap housing, and just over the river were the amusements of Asakusa Park, but despite this, a surprisingly large area of scrubland remained, as well as several derelict huts around a solitary fishing pond. It was a strange mixture of clutter and quiet. On one corner of the neighborhood stood a rotting old mansion with the look of a haunted house (this story takes place a little before the great earthquake of 1923). It was this building that Masaki had noticed in passing one day and decided to lease out.

The property had a large garden covered with thick weeds that was surrounded by a hedge and crumbling earthen walls. In the middle stood a clay-walled storehouse seemingly on the point of collapse. A little to the side was the main house - quite grand, but so decrepit as to be almost uninhabitable - but for Masaki, this building was of little interest. The attraction for moving here was entirely down to that old storehouse. The feeling of being alone, protected by its thick walls from the dazzling sunlight and outside clamor, with the rich aroma of camphor in the air, was something he'd always longed for. In the same way a courtesan might hide her face behind a veil, all Masaki wanted was to shelter from the world's gaze within those walls.

He laid out tatami mats on the second floor of the building and brought in his cherished library of eccentric books - as well as life-sized Buddhist statues carved from wood, several pale *Noh* masks, and other items he had purchased from an antique shop in Yokohama - creating his own strange cell. The only source of natural light was from two small iron-framed windows facing north and south. In order to make the space even more gloomy,

Masaki kept the metal shutter on the southern window tightly closed, so all year round no direct sunlight ever entered. This was his living room, his study, and bedroom.

On the ground floor he left the bare floorboards as they were, and here, messily crammed in, stacked one on top of another were all his other worldly possessions: red lacquered chests that had been passed down through generations; imposing wardrobes with locks bearing elaborate family crests; worm riddled boxes of old armor; bookcases filled with worthless copies; and all sorts of other brick-a-brac and junk.

In the main house he replaced the tatami mats in the hall, which was about 15 square meters in size, and laid this out as a reception area for guests (who rarely ever came). He also replaced the mats in a room next to the kitchen, about six square meters in size, which would serve as living quarters for the old lady he employed as a cook. He told this elderly lady not to approach the entrance to the storehouse, where he fitted locks inside and out to its sturdy door, so whether he was there or not the building could be firmly secured. It was now, in a manner of speaking, like one of those forbidden rooms found in ghost stories.

The cook matched Masaki's needs perfectly. She had no relatives, and although 65-years-old her hearing was still good and she suffered from no ailments to speak of. She kept herself well presented and was very diligent in her work. But most happily for Masaki, unlike many women her age and in her position, she had a breezy, light-hearted nature, and was not at all suspicious or inquisitive about her master or what he got up to inside that old storehouse. She seemed perfectly happy to collect her pay at the end of each month, and engage herself in flower arranging or visiting the temple when not preparing meals.

I need not mention that Masaki spent almost all his time in that room on the second floor, where the light was so dim it was impossible to tell if it was afternoon or evening. He would while away whole days flicking through the yellowing pages of some work from his library, or lying on his back in the middle of the floor and gazing at the Buddhist statues or *Noh* masks on the wall, lost in mystical visions. Before long it would be night, and through the single small window above him the velvet sky and twinkling stars would appear like an illustration from a children's fairy tale.

When it got too dark he occasionally lit a candle on his desk and sat and read, or wrote bizarre compositions late into the night. On most evenings though it was his habit to leave the storehouse and wander into town. It may seem odd that someone with such an intense dislike of other people would enjoy walking around such lively areas of the city, but nevertheless more often than not he would head for the bustling Asakusa Park just across the river. Although, perhaps it was exactly because of his misanthropy that he loved the anonymous nature of the crowds he found there, where nobody spoke or looked at you for long. For him the crowd was no more than a picture or puppet show, to be observed detachedly. Being jostled among hordes of people meant he could disappear even more effectively from the world's gaze than when he was alone in his storehouse. Masaki was able vanish in a crowd of strangers; it was his cloak of invisibility. He especially targeted the swarms of theater goers that poured out of venue doors at the end of each show. By walking among this throng he could distract himself from his own solitude, in much the same way as the title character in Edgar Allan Poe's short story "The Man of the Crowd".

But now, let me return to Masaki's reunion with Fuyuo Kinoshita which I mentioned at the beginning of this story. This came two years after Masaki had moved into that old storehouse, shortly after the start of spring. Their meeting was a hugely significant event for Masaki, shattering his calm, eccentric way of life, as if a stone had been hurled into the still waters of his settled world.

2

As I said earlier, the deeply misanthropic Masaki had one friend. This was a young gentleman by the name of Ikeuchi Koutarou, a manager at a trading company - a job he got thanks to the influence of his father who was quite well known in the business community. Masaki and Ikeuchi were the same age but completely different in every other way. Ikeuchi was cheerful and gregarious. He never thought too deeply about anything, but on the other hand was perceptive and quick-witted. He was well liked and good company. The two had been friends since they were young as their families lived near each other and they attended the same elementary school. When they reached adolescence Masaki's odd ideas and strange behavior baffled Ikeuchi but this only drew him closer. He gave more credit to Masaki's habits than they deserved, and even felt a kind of pride in having such a philosophical companion. Disregarding Masaki's attempts to avoid him, Ikeuchi often visited his home, and engaged him in playful irrelevant debates. Masaki's gloomy study and Masaki himself offered an escape or an oasis for Ikeuchi, who had grown accustomed to regular society.

One day Masaki was entertaining Ikeuchi in the reception room of his new house (even his one and only friend was not allowed entry to the storehouse) and while Ikeuchi was chatting about his colorful social life, he turned to his friend with a smile and said: "You know recently I've become quite well acquainted with a rather beautiful young actress called Fuyuo Kinoshita."

His smile seemed to suggest something more meaningful behind the words "well acquainted". He went on: "But listen, this should interest you, Fuyuo's real name is actually Fumiko Kinoshita. Sounds familiar right? She was that pretty honor student we used to tease in school. The one who was a couple of years below us."

Masaki gave a start when he heard this name and felt his face flush slightly. Although the 27-year-old Masaki had not blushed in a long time, as soon as he realized his cheeks were turning red he couldn't stop them from growing hotter and hotter, just like when he was a child and the more he tried to hide his tears the more they would flow. "Was there really such a girl with that name? Well maybe, but I guess I wasn't quite as precocious as you." Masaki tried to hide his embarrassment as he spoke. Luckily the room was quite dark so it seemed Ikeuchi had not noticed his discomfort.

"Come now, you must remember", his friend objected, "she was known throughout school for her looks. Say, why don't you come to the theater with me one time and see for yourself. She hasn't changed a bit so you're sure to recognize her." Clearly Ikeuchi was rather proud of his association with the actress.

Masaki had not known she was working under a pseudonym but he certainly remembered Fumiko Kinoshita, and it was only natural he should blush at the mention of her name. As I've said before Masaki was an intensely shy child, but that's not to say he wasn't mature for his age. In fact, at an earlier stage than most of his contemporaries he developed a kind of youthful longing for the female students in his school, and from fourth grade all the way to twelfth, he harbored such feelings towards Fumiko. Although he never played the kind of pranks Ikeuchi did, such as making the girl cry on the way home from school by pulling at the ribbons in her hair - the most he could do was wrap himself in his own hot arms and sigh deeply when he was off school with a cold, and turn his feverish imagination to Fumiko's sweet smile.

One day the young Masaki was gifted with a rather perverse opportunity. When he was in 11th grade one of his classmates, a stocky boy with a wispy mustache, decided to send a note to Fumiko signaling his affections (she was in 9th grade at the time) and told Masaki to write it. This unruly youth was the neighborhood bully and as the weakest member of the class Masaki was terrified of him. The boy just had to tap him on the shoulder and say "Come" and his eyes would well up in the usual way. He had no choice but to immediately give in to the order, and when he came home from school that day he put all his effort into the troublesome task, skipping his usual snack and going straight to his room. He unrolled a sheet of writing paper on his desk and began to rack his brains over how to draft his first ever love letter. As he began to pen some early lines, an odd notion occurred to him.

That brute will be the one handing this letter to Fumiko, but I am the one writing it. I can put down how I truly feel and she

will read these words. Even though she won't realize it is from me, as I sit here and picture her beauty I can confess my innermost feelings.
Masaki got carried away by this idea, and spent several hours pouring his heart out, even blotting the pages with his own tears. The next day the bully gave the thick sheaf of notes to Fumiko, but it turned out they were most likely chucked on the fire by her mother, as afterwards there was no change in the naturally cheerful girl, and even the bully soon acted as if nothing had happened. Only the letter writer, Masaki, continued to dwell on the incident and the discarded words he had vainly fretted over. In writing the letter his feelings had deepened, and life had become near unbearable for him, so he hatched a plan. One day he waited until no one was around then crept into Fumiko's classroom. He lifted the lid of her desk and took the smallest, most worn out pencil he could find from her pencil case. When he got home he solemnly cleaned out a drawer in the small wardrobe in his room, wrapped the pencil in paper and enshrined it there, as though it were a sacred relic. Whenever his loneliness became too much, he would open the drawer and kneel down in worship. Fumiko had become no less than a goddess.
Later on, as is the way of things, the girl moved out of the area, Masaki changed school, and before he knew it he had forgotten about her. But now, hearing her name being spoken again by Ikeuchi, it all came back to him. Although his friend knew nothing of this episode, he blushed deeply from the shame.
Because Masaki was the type who enjoyed the solitude of crowds - such as those in Asakusa Park - he also liked the anonymity of a packed train, or a theater audience, and so had a reasonable knowledge of the latest plays being staged. Although Fuyuo Kinoshita had previously only been on the fringes of the theatrical scene, she had recently joined a popular troupe of performers who put on modern *Shingeki* dramas, and her stock had suddenly risen. She wasn't the leading actress, but she'd made a name for herself thanks to her spellbinding beauty and physical allure, and occupied a special position just below the

principal. Masaki had not seen her performing yet, but was aware of her reputation. When he found out this Fuyuo was actually Fumiko his first love, even the misanthropic Masaki couldn't help being thrilled, and he began to feel a nostalgic ache. Although a little apprehensive, he made up his mind to see her. He did not mind so much that she was involved with Ikeuchi, as Masaki was incapable of true love anyway.

It was three or four days later that the pair of them went to the K theater to see Fuyuo Kinoshita perform. Luckily, or perhaps unluckily for Masaki, the leading actress happened to be ill that night, and Fuyuo took on the main role of Salome - and what a voluptuous enchantress she had become. That pretty young girl with braided hair, that innocent angel, the holy virgin that Masaki had worshiped, was now a stunningly beautiful woman. Her distinctive large eyes, delicate chin, and trembling lips so full and round, all had an unforgettable sexual attraction - even more so when her face broke into a graceful smile. At first Masaki felt an almost oppressive terror in her presence, but this soon turned to wonder, then longing, then a burning desire. Seeing her with adult eyes, the grown-up Fumiko was no longer sacred. Shamefully, and unwittingly, Masaki began to defile her image in his mind. He mentally caressed this vision, held it in his arms, and violently struck at it. This fantasy was influenced in part by the vulgar commentary provided by Ikeuchi in the next seat, who kept whispering in his ear.

The tale of Salome was the last act of that evening's entertainment, and when this was over Masaki and Ikeuchi left the theater and climbed into a cab. With a knowing wink, Ikeuchi gave the name of a nearby restaurant to the driver. Masaki realized what he was up to, but offered no objection. The spectacle of Fuyuo as Salome had overwhelmed and entranced him, and he had to see her again in the flesh.

The two friends were half-heartedly exchanging their views on the theater in one of the restaurant's large private rooms when Fuyuo appeared, now dressed in a kimono. She stood outside the open sliding door and laughed pleasantly at Ikeuchi's upturned face. When she spotted Masaki though, her expression changed to one of uncertainty, and she looked to Ikeuchi for an explanation.

"Fuyuo, don't you remember this gentleman?", he asked with a mischievous grin.

She stared at Masaki. "Well...now."

"It's my old friend, Masaki Aizou, my classmate from school. Back then people used to say he had a thing for you."

"My, of course, Masaki, now I recognize you. How wonderful to see you after all these years. You look just the same. I suppose I've changed considerably though." Her coquettish charm in that moment, as she bowed politely, was something Masaki would never forget. "I remember you being the brightest boy in the whole school - and nothing like Ikeuchi here who used to tease me terribly and make me cry."

Masaki was transfixed. It seemed even the charming Ikeuchi could be no match for this beguiling woman. The topic of conversation soon drifted from their school days to the theater. As he drank, Ikeuchi showed off his expertise in the subject. His theories were certainly eloquent and well thought out, but just like his views on philosophy, they remained superficial. Fuyuo, also a little tipsy, picked at the main points of his argument, each time casting a glance at Masaki. Her attitude seemed to suggest she felt Masaki (although he was no expert) had a deeper grasp of the subject, and while she toyed with Ikeuchi, she took everything Masaki said as gospel. The inexperienced Masaki was delighted with her surprising conviviality and became unusually talkative. Although his way of speaking was often a little difficult for her to follow, when he got into his stride, Fuyuo would gaze into his eyes with a look of near total admiration. When it was time to leave she said to him in all seriousness, without a hint of false flattery, "I hope from now you will grace me with your company again, and it will be just as educational."

Ikeuchi had perhaps hoped this reunion would create some mischief, but instead it must have stirred up unexpected feelings of jealousy. For Masaki, Fuyuo had shown a quaint, contemplative side - most unlike that of someone in the acting profession - and this had made her even more desirable.

I remember you being the brightest boy in the whole school - as he rode the tram home, like a child he repeated her words over and over to himself.

3

It was six months after this that Masaki Aizou came to brutally murder the actress Fuyuo Kinoshita. During those six months the two met only three more times - these occasions coming in the same month after that first night in the restaurant - so her murder actually took place five months after they last met. No one could have suspected Masaki of being the killer, when it seemed for those five months they had completely forgotten each other's existence. The period of time between possible motive and the shocking crime itself was too vast, and the two could not be connected (which is why Masaki was able to avoid the attentions of the police). But of course that is only how it appeared. In fact during those five months Masaki frequently saw Fuyuo, at a rate of more than once a week, albeit through unconventional methods. So for him at least, his murderous urge grew quite naturally, and the path he took entirely expected.

Fuyuo was Masaki's first love. As a child he had fetishized her possessions, worshiped them as sacred relics. Now, some ten years later, his mind had been sent reeling once again by her bewitching stage presence, and then - although he'd never spoken to her during their school days - they'd spent time together in friendly conversation. She'd smiled at him and listened intently to his theories with almost reverential admiration. For the misanthropic and cowardly Masaki this was all too much; he was powerless against such charm. She had an irresistible hold over him unlike that of any woman. Three evenings were all it took for him to become completely infatuated again.

That third meeting was at a different location to their first, but the party members were the same. As usual Ikeuchi invited him along as an extra dinner companion, but Masaki secretly flattered himself that Fuyuo's willingness to join them was only because she knew he would be there. "Poor Ikeuchi", he'd thought. Each time they met, the way she acted towards his friend was typical of certain popular actresses. She mocked and patronized him, almost to the point of cruelty. This intimidated Masaki and made her appear exactly the kind of woman he feared. But her attitude towards him was completely different. Fuyuo became his disciple; she clung to his every word. And it seemed her affections were only deepening the more they saw of each other.

But Masaki had entirely misunderstood the situation. Fuyuo was the kind of woman who could skillfully display two or three different sides to her character depending on the occasion or the person she was with, like a dancer switching between two masks. She regarded Masaki in the same way Ikeuchi saw him. His gloomy introspection interested her, as if he were a character from a 19th century novel, and she admired his opinions on art and theater. But her affection for him went no further. Masaki was completely oblivious to this, and in his conceit pitied Ikeuchi - while Ikeuchi secretly sneered at Masaki's naivety. It was Ikeuchi's intention from the start to take malicious pleasure in flaunting his new mistress before his adorable but guileless friend. But now Masaki had fulfilled his purpose he had become something of a nuisance. He was also beginning to display a kind of creepy eagerness which bothered Ikeuchi, and even though he wasn't aware of his friend's shameful idolization of Fuyuo during their schooldays, he decided it was time to bring an end to his fun.

That third time they had dinner they made plans to visit the seaside town of Kamakura. As it happened Fuyuo would be free the following Sunday, so they fixed on this date when they parted that evening. Masaki then waited impatiently for Ikeuchi to send further details, but no word came. He telegrammed him but there was no reply, and before long, the appointed day came and went. As Masaki had already guessed Ikeuchi and Fuyuo were more than friends he speculated jealousy was to blame for Ikeuchi's silence. He actually took some vain pride in the notion that such a witty and handsome man could be envious of someone like him. The betrayal however still left him at a loss. As the days dragged on, without any contact with Fuyuo, Masaki became more and more restless. He would watch her perform two or three times a week from the upper circle of the theater, hidden in the crowd, but this was no consolation and only made him more desperate to meet her again. Most of the time he'd hide away on the second floor of his storehouse for whole days and nights, lost in visions of the actress. He covered his eyes and in the darkness her figure would appear, close-up, writhing seductively. Her pure, angelic schoolgirl smile would transform into the coquettish smirk of the half naked Salome, the golden cloth covering her sumptuous bosom rising and falling like waves as she sighed, her two powerful arms twisting like snakes as she danced - then she was kneeling, dressed in her kimono, its fabric stretched tight suppressing her savage sexuality. She was looking up at him as he spoke, and he examined her body minutely from every angle, his mind whirling deliriously. It's hard to imagine or explain his infatuation, when even the wooden Buddhist statue standing in the corner of the room became a subject of his carnal fantasies.

One evening he could stand it no longer and decided he had to act. Despite his solitary nature he always dressed fashionably whenever he went out, and that night would be no exception. He told the old cook to run him a bath, then he washed and shaved, changed into an elegant suit, and made his way to Azumabashi Bridge where he picked up a cab to S theater - where Fuyuo's current show was playing. He'd been thinking about doing this for a while, so knew by the time the cab pulled up outside the stage door the performance would be just finishing. He told the driver to wait, then got out and stood by the steps to the artists' entrance where the actors emerged after removing their stage make-up. Once before, he and Ikeuchi had met Fuyuo this way, so he was familiar with the scene before him. Milling around were groups of young girls hoping to catch a glimpse of their favorite actor, while sharply dressed young hoodlums mingled among them. Masaki noticed an older gentleman in the crowd who also seemed to have a car waiting for him and who kept his eyes fixed on the stage door.

For half an hour Masaki patiently endured his embarrassment, then finally Fuyuo appeared, dressed in a kimono coming down the steps. In his haste he stumbled as he moved towards her, and just as he was about to call her name, the older gentleman approached from the other side and spoke to the actress as if they were old friends. Like a dull-witted child Masaki turned red and lost even the courage to retreat. He just stood there dumbly, watching the couple talk. The gentlemen kept pointing to his car and inviting Fuyuo to join him. He seemed to know her well as she was happy to accept his invitation and began walking towards the vehicle when finally her distinctive large eyes spotted Masaki. "My, it's Masaki isn't it?"

Hearing her say his name Masaki felt like he'd been pulled out of a dark pit. "Yes, I just happened to be passing, and wondered if I could give you a lift."

Ignoring the gentlemen she had just been speaking to, Fuyuo replied in an overly familiar way: "Oh, is that so. Well in that case, I would be much obliged. Actually I was hoping to run into you anyway." She then bluntly apologized to the older man and walked with Masaki to his car talking as she went. Rather than feeling pleased with himself, Masaki was stunned that this magnificent creature should be so amiable, and tripping over his words, he gave the driver Fuyuo's address.

"It was awful of Ikeuchi to allow our plans for that Sunday to come to nothing, I hope it didn't inconvenience you too much." Fuyuo remarked as the sudden motion of the car brought their bodies closer together. She'd been seeing Ikeuchi almost every other day since then, so her words were purely for effect. Masaki, feeling Fuyuo's warmth beside him, replied timidly that it was she who must have been inconvenienced, and Fuyuo suggested they should all go somewhere at the end of the month.

When they had lapsed into silence, feeling only each other's presence, the car interior suddenly lit up - they had arrived at a main road with bright streetlights and signs, and gleaming shop windows. Fuyuo muttered softly "My, how dazzling" and promptly pulled the shade down on her side of the car, then asked Masaki to do the same. There was no hidden intent in this. As a young woman in the acting profession she tired of being in the public eye, and often lowered the window shades when alone. When with a man she was even more careful to do so. All the same, this was perhaps a sign that she underestimated Masaki. He on the other hand couldn't help misconstrue the meaning of her actions. He foolishly convinced himself she was deliberately handing him an opening. Trembling, he pulled down every shade, then for what felt like an age, sat facing directly forward without moving a muscle.

"You can raise them again now," Fuyuo said a little awkwardly as they had now entered a dimly lit part of town, but her words only encouraged Masaki to finally make his move. His whole body twitched slightly, then without speaking, he placed his hand over Fuyuo's, which was resting on her knee, then gradually began to apply more pressure. Realizing Masaki's intentions, Fuyuo skillfully slipped her hand from underneath his, and shifted towards the corner of her seat. She then stared intently at his frozen expression; his face now seemed to be carved from wood. Suddenly, unexpectedly, she laughed. But more than just a snigger, she roared and howled. In all his life Masaki had never heard a laugh like it. It continued on, and on, longer than seemed possible. The memory of that laugh might have been able to bear, but what he couldn't endure was that he laughed too. What a detestable sound that was! In his attempt to cover up the incident by acting as if it had all been a joke he only made it more shameful. All he could do was shudder at the thought of his own gullibility.

It is perhaps not so absurd to suggest the murderous passion that led Masaki to eventually commit his atrocious act must have taken root, not with Fuyuo's laugh, but with his own.

4

For several days after this Masaki sat around the second floor of his storehouse in a daze. He felt more keenly than ever the impenetrable barrier between himself and others. His hatred of humanity welled up like a kind of nausea. He especially despised Fuyuo, seeing her as representative of all womankind. But by some strange action of the heart, while loathing her intensely, he couldn't forget how he'd felt during their schooldays. He also couldn't forget her alluring eyes, her lips, her body - it was clear he was besotted with the actress - and even more so since his humiliation. His ardent desire and deep resentment dissolved into one. If they ever met again, the shame and abhorrence he'd feel would be too much to bear - but even so, he never stopped wanting her.

It may seem odd since he despised Fuyuo so much that Masaki continued to secretly watch her perform, hidden in the back seats of the theater. Like all misanthropes, in contrast to his extreme anxiety at being seen or heard by others, he reveled in those places away from the gaze of strangers (or at least places where his existence was not noticed such as the crowds of Asakusa Park). One reason Masaki shut himself away in that old storehouse was so he could indulge himself in all the selfish behavior he suppressed when in the company of others (this love of secrecy is something the misanthrope and the vicious criminal have in common). Masaki's animosity towards Fuyuo drew from the sickening humiliation he felt when they were last face-to-face. But since he could observe her from his seat in the packed theater without any danger of being seen himself, there was no contradiction in his presence there.

However, simply watching Fuyuo perform on stage did not ease Masaki's lovelorn soul. In fact the more he saw her, the more his unquenchable desire intensified, until finally he was led to commit his murderous act. A decisive moment in this came one evening when he was leaving the theater after seeing Fuyuo's show, and - perhaps provoked by the thought of that night in the cab - was suddenly struck by a desire to catch another glimpse of her in the flesh. Lost in the darkness and the crowds, he silently moved in the direction of the stage door. As he turned the corner of the building something unexpected made him slink back into the shadows. There, by the steps to the artists' entrance, standing among the throng of people, was Ikeuchi Koutarou. Acting like a private detective Masaki kept watch on his friend, taking great care not to be spotted himself. After a while Fuyuo came down the steps and Ikeuchi went to meet her. They stood together for a moment and talked. It was clear Ikeuchi had a car waiting and he was to escort the actress somewhere.

Although Masaki had already supposed from Fuyuo's reaction the other night that her relationship with Ikeuchi had developed further, seeing them together with his own eyes filled him with a terrible jealousy. He instinctively decided to follow them, and hurriedly hailed a nearby cab, ordering the driver to stay close to Ikeuchi's car. The driver did as he was told, keeping it within range of his own headlights. There was no sign Ikeuchi realized he was being followed - viewed from behind his car bounced along innocently, then after a short while the shades of its rear window were pulled down just like that night with Masaki - though this time it signified something very different which aggravated him terribly.

Ikeuchi's car came to a stop outside the gates of a hotel in the Tsukiji district. It seemed like the perfect location for a lover's tryst - hidden behind a lush front garden it had a quiet, upmarket appearance. The couple's deliberate care not to be seen in public annoyed Masaki even further. He watched as they entered the hotel, then he got out of his cab and vacantly walked up and down in front of the building. Agitated to the point of delirium with love, envy, and rage, he had no intention of leaving. After almost an hour of restless pacing he suddenly made up his mind and walked through the gates. Although the receptionist made it clear they preferred only regular patrons, he insisted, and booked himself in for the night. The hotel was large but it was late and there were few guests around so it had a gloomy, deserted air. Masaki went straight up to his room on the second floor and had his bed made up, then lay down and waited for the hour to grow even later.

When the large clock in the corridor chimed two o'clock Masaki quickly got to his feet, and still in his nightclothes slipped out into the silent hallway. Moving against the walls like a shadow, he sought out Ikeuchi and Fuyuo's room. It was an extremely arduous task. Barefoot, taking more care than a cat burglar, he inched open the paneled sliding door of each room he came to, until eventually finding the one he was looking for. The lights were off but he could hear the whisper of voices - and he knew straight away it was Fuyuo and Ikeuchi. Aware that the couple were still awake, Masaki had to be more cautious than ever. Calming his racing heart, he pressed himself up against the door, and strained to listen with every fiber of his body. Since it would never have occurred to Fuyuo and Ikeuchi that Masaki was eavesdropping they spoke without restraint, although at a low whisper. Their talk didn't concern anything significant, but for Masaki, to hear Fuyuo speaking so openly, using such rough language, in that familiar purring voice, was almost too much to bear. And yet there he remained - craning his neck, holding his breath, staying as stiff as a statue, so not one sound from inside that room escaped him, listening, listening, his bloodshot eyes staring off into space.

5

It's no exaggeration to say that from this moment on, and for the next five months until his terrible crime, Masaki's life consisted entirely of tailing, eavesdropping, and spying on Ikeuchi Koutarou and Fuyuo Kinoshita. He hovered around their liaisons like an eerie silhouette. Although he had pictured their love making before, to now actually catch them in the act was an unbearable humiliation that caused him a hollow melancholy he had never known. He was struck by an almost physical pain. Standing behind that sliding door, hearing Ikeuchi's pressuring, coaxing tone, made Masaki blush with intense shame. The sound of Fuyuo's voice, frank, and vulgar, using language unthinkable for a woman in the daytime, caused his skin to bristle, while her familiar sweet whisper made his eyes fill with hot tears. Then, when he heard the rustle of silk, and the hint of a sigh, he lost all feeling below his knees and his legs trembled from the horror he felt.

Alone in the darkness on the other side of that door, Masaki experienced every kind of shame and fury - and yet he drank it all in. If he'd been a normal individual, he would never have gone on to repeat this agony. Or rather, he wouldn't have plotted such a villainous deed as eavesdropping in the first place. But Masaki was not a normal individual (in fact, not only did he have the introverted, misanthropic personality of an outsider, there was also some detestable peculiarity, perhaps hidden in another of his traits - his strange obsession with secrets and sin - and it was this latent capacity for evil that was suddenly awoken by his singular experience).

Such despicably secretive behavior led Masaki to feel a creeping guilt, a rage that almost brought him to tears, a terror that set his teeth on edge, but strange as it may seem, also a boundless joy and indescribable intoxication. He could not resist the savage charm of the unexpected world he had peeked into - and this utterly bizarre way of life became Masaki's normality. He devoted every hour of the day to investigating the time and place of Ikeuchi and Fuyuo's liaisons. He never missed an opportunity to follow them, listen in on their conversations, and peek at their love making. It so happened that during this period the lovers' relationship became ever more intimate, and their trysts grew more frequent. The more enchanted they became with each other, the more fervently Masaki drifted back and forth across that intricate boundary between pleasure and pain. Again and again, his frustration growing and intensifying.

In most cases, each time Ikeuchi and Fuyuo separated Masaki got a clue as to their next rendezvous - the location would not necessarily be the hotel in Tsukiji, and they did not always meet at the stage door to Fuyuo's theater - but wherever they met Masaki was always there hanging around like a malevolent shadow - lodging at the same hotel, observing their every move, either from outside their door or in the next room, even sometimes making a small peephole in the wall separating them (one can only imagine the great pains he must have gone through to ensure he was never discovered). In this way, sometimes clearly, sometimes only dimly, he saw the lovers' every gesture, and heard their every word.

On one such evening Masaki was listening to the pair as they talked quietly when Ikeuchi suddenly exclaimed: "Don't blame me for what happened, I'm not Masaki Aizou", and Fuyuo responded by laughing: "Ha, how true! You may be a hopeless case but you're adorable at least. That egghead Masaki makes my skin crawl. To think anyone could fall for such a guileless blockhead."

Fuyuo's laugh was low, but its arrogant tone pierced Masaki's heart like a drill. It was exactly the same laugh as that evening inside the cab. All Masaki could think of was that impenetrable wall, merciless and cruel. Hearing the unguarded, indulgent gossip of these two lovers, Masaki was forced to face the truth - he was not like other people, he was an outsider and completely alone in this world. Gradually a train of thought developed in his mind.

I am a different species. That's why I'm suited to such vile, disgusting behavior. The sins of this world do not apply to me. For a creature like myself, this is my only path.

But then, the more he spied on Fuyuo, the more fiercely his desire burned for her, until he had to gasp for breath. Each time he secretly observed her body he discovered some new enchantment. More than once he gazed at her dim white form writhing in the semi-darkness as he peered through the narrow gap in the door to her room. Lying under a mosquito net (by now the summer had come) wearing only a thin silk gauze dressing gown, she was like a mermaid at the bottom of the ocean. On such occasions, her appearance brought back dreamlike wistful memories of his mother, or rather she exuded a mystical beauty both subtle and profound.

On other occasions she took a very different form, becoming a delirious temptress - the twirling locks of her hair like hundreds of snakes twisting together as she flung her kimono aside, her naked body dazzling with a pink radiance, the luster of her skin shimmering in the air. Such a savage spectacle was too much for Masaki who would tremble all over.

One evening when Masaki was staying in the room next to the lovers - while the couple were out using the bathroom - he managed to make a small hole in the paper skirting at the bottom of the sand-coated wall separating them using a pointed fire iron. Enthralled by this technique, from that night onwards he did his best to always secure a neighboring room - then whatever the hotel, he made sure to fashion a peephole to look through. It occurred to Masaki just how corrupted he'd become, but even though he was shocked and mortified by his own devious behavior, he felt no remorse. He was consumed by a monstrous lust, relentless and brazen, just like the love-obsessed priest *Seigen* in "The story of Sakurahime".

Masaki would awkwardly crouch down on his hands and knees and press his nose against the wall, then patiently peer through the small hole. On the other side, a gorgeously grotesque picture of hell would be laid out, enveloping him in a bewitching haze. Once, the nape of Fuyuo's neck filled his vision, spreading out like a lustrous white wall causing the blood to pound in his veins. Another time, the soft underside of her foot blocked his view, the skin creased like the face of an old man, wrinkled in laughter. But what consumed Masaki most, above all these enchantments, were the faint dark-red scratches tinged with blood on Fuyuo's calves. These were perhaps caused by Ikeuchi's nails, Masaki wasn't sure, but the curiously beautiful contrast between the almost dazzling luster of Fuyuo's peach colored flesh - as her calves wriggled and extended before his eyes - and the cruel, vividly marked cuts on her skin, produced images that Masaki would never forget.

Even though he felt a freakish thrill from his uncouth behavior - along with the humiliation and anguish - as the days went by Masaki became more embittered and fretful, and his mind began to unravel. Although he was mere inches away when he listened to Fuyuo's voice from the other side of a hotel wall, there was still a limitless gap between them. Although her body was so close, he could never hold her, embrace her, or touch her at all. And what's more, right before Masaki's eyes Ikeuchi was able to do all these things, seemingly so casually and freely.

Unable to withstand this cruel and unusual torment it was only natural that Masaki would finally entertain his horrifying notion. It was an absurd and insane course of action, but the only one left open to him. Nothing else could fulfill his desire.

6

It was two months after he began following Fuyuo and Ikeuchi that a malicious voice began muttering unearthly thoughts in Masaki's ear. For two or three weeks he was slowly drawn in by this enticing whisper, until he finally fixed on a concrete plan that left no room for turning back.

One evening Masaki made a rare visit to Ikeuchi Koutarou's home. Masaki's recent covert activities meant he'd frequently observed his friend but Ikeuchi hadn't seen Masaki for a month and a half, so for him the meeting was a little awkward. Taking some care and employing his usual clever manner of speech Ikeuchi claimed not to have seen Fuyuo since they last met, and glossed over recent events. Masaki though had been waiting for Fuyuo's name to come up and took this opportunity to confess casually: "Since we're talking about that actress there is a small matter I should apologize for. It's perhaps nothing really, but the truth is, over a month or so ago when Fuyuo was appearing at the S theater, I happened to be passing when her show finished, so I decided to wait outside the stage door and give her a lift home. Inside the cab, purely on a whim, I made a pass at her - but you have no reason to get angry - she turned me down flat. I'm afraid she was too much for me to handle. I'm sorry to have kept this from you, I guess even now I'm a little envious of your relationship with that woman. It's regrettable, and hard to admit to such a pathetic story, but I felt I had to own up. As I say it was just a whim, I've no intention of seeing her again. You know yourself, I'm not capable of true affection."

Masaki himself did not clearly understand why he had to confess to Ikeuchi, but keeping this secret had felt wrong somehow - admitting to the sorry episode on the other hand brought a kind of relief.

Without exception, all madmen will believe that it is everyone else - all rational ordinary people - who are in fact insane. And so Aizou Masaki's conviction that the rest of humanity was an alien species is perhaps evidence that his misanthropy from the very beginning was a kind of lunacy. In truth, he was already mad. His persistent and brazen acts of covert surveillance were certainly signs of a warped mind. But what he did next was even more absurd - this introspective, anti-social loner, enrolled himself in a driving school.

The school in question was upstream along the Sumida river and he began traveling there each day without fail. What's more, he earnestly meant this as an essential part of the terrible plan that had formed in his mind.

He wrote about his lessons in the following letter to Ikeuchi:

"Lately I've taken up a rather unusual pastime. As you know I'm a gloomy, old-fashioned sort, so if I said I'd started learning to drive, no doubt you'd be very surprised. Well, each morning I've been getting up early, quite unlike me, and heading straight to a driving school, which has rather shocked my old cook. Strangely enough I'm actually getting the hang of it - day after day, fooling around in an old beat up Ford they use as a practice vehicle - at this rate after another month I should be able to get my license. If all goes well I intend to buy myself a car then go on jaunts around the city. It's perfect for me - roaming around Tokyo at high speed, sitting in a box on my own, without anyone paying me any attention. As you know, what I hate most about going out is the unbearable feeling of being looked at. Even in a cab you have to speak to the driver and give directions. At the very least they have to know where you are going. But if I drive myself nobody has to know. I can have the same feeling I have when I am holed up in my storehouse, and yet be able to prowl about all over the place. No matter how lively the street or how congested, I can pass through completely at ease, like a hermit wrapped in a cloak of invisibility. Is this not the ideal mode of transport for someone like me? I must say I'm like a kid before Christmas, I can't wait to pass my test."

Boldly exposing part of his preparations for the crime he was about to commit was a deliberate all-or-nothing strategy by Masaki to throw Ikeuchi off-guard and allay his friend's suspicions. Masaki knew that by dressing up this daring disclosure as nothing more than idle amusement, Ikeuchi was more likely to be put at ease. Of course because Masaki continued his regular spying he was able to pay close attention to his friend's demeanour, but after receiving this letter Ikeuchi only seemed amused by Masaki's eccentricity and suspected nothing.

After only about a month's practice, at quite some expense, Masaki successfully acquired a driving license. At the same time, with the school's help, he bought a second-hand box-type Ford. One reason he chose this rather cheap model was to save money, but mainly it was so he could blend in with the rest of the Tokyo traffic as most of the cabs in use at the time were of a similar type. He also made sure to have new shades fitted to the back seat windows. Next he had a garage built, which was no problem at all since as I mentioned before he had a large overgrown garden at his disposal. Once this was finished Masaki shut himself inside for two whole nights and played the role of carpenter, making up some excuse to keep his old cook away. During this time he removed the passenger seats at the back of the car, put in wooden planks in the space left behind, then refitted the cushions so there was now a box large enough for a single person to fit in when lying down. In effect he had built a coffin-shaped space underneath, impossible to spot from the outside.

After Masaki had completed this odd task, he visited various second-hand clothes shops and bought a high-collared suit, of the type worn by cab drivers, a tweed overcoat and a large peaked cap which covered his eyes. Putting on this outfit, he began to go for drives at all times of the day around central Tokyo and the suburbs.

What a truly bizarre sight this was - a wild and unkempt garden overgrown with weeds; an old storehouse with crumbling walls; a derelict mansion on the point of collapse; then emerging from the gates of this bleak haunted house, a splendid looking automobile - even if only a second-hand Ford - slipping out day after day to some unknown destination - and when the hour was late, its headlights flashing like the eyes of some monstrous creature. Rumors spread, and the old cook and nearby residents couldn't help keeping watch for this eccentric spectacle.

Delighted that he'd learnt to drive in only a month, Masaki - dressed up in his driver's costume - became more and more reckless in his aimless jaunts. He explored the town center and as long as the roads were drivable traveled all over the city outskirts. Once he parked the car by the gates of Ikeuchi's office and invited his astonished friend out for a tour, going from the gardens of the Imperial Palace to around Ueno Park.

"This kind of stunt isn't like you at all - but these old Fords *are* perhaps your style", Ikeuchi had said, looking considerably surprised. When Masaki thought about how shocked his friend would be if he knew a dead body would soon be hidden in the space under his seat - he had to crouch forward as he drove to stifle his laughter against his shoulder.

On another occasion he brazenly followed Fuyuo as she walked along the street - though he only tried this trick once - amusing himself in this way was extremely risky, if she'd spotted him his whole plan would have come to naught. Then again, it was the danger that made it so thrilling. What a comical and yet sinister scene - a beautiful young woman in western dress swaggering down the sidewalk, and a beat-up old Ford crawling along some distance behind her. Each time she turned a corner the Ford would turn too, like a dog on a lead. And Masaki in the driver's seat, grinning weirdly, singing softly to himself, "Hey young lady, your coffin is here, following right behind you".

Masaki patiently waited a month after buying his car so no-one - Ikeuchi, the old cook and the neighbors included - would realize the real reason for his purchase. He thought it would be suspicious if no sooner had he bought the Ford than Fuyuo disappeared - though perhaps he was being unnecessarily careful. On the surface it must have seemed to everyone that Masaki and Fuyuo were simply two people who vaguely knew each other from school who happened to meet again after ten years and have dinner three or four times - all this happening several months ago. Nobody could have made the connection between Masaki buying a car and Fuyuo being murdered, even if these two events occurred on exactly the same day. Nevertheless, the deeply cautious Masaki whiled away a month cruising around town before finally deciding to make his move - although there were two or three small matters to take care of first: such as getting the printed sticker with the red mark of a Tokyo cab; acquiring a false license plate for the car; and preparing a grave for Fuyuo's body. He was able to get hold of the first two items without much trouble, and had the perfect solution for the third. Masaki knew there was a deep, dried up old well in the middle of his garden, so one day he took a stroll in the grounds of his house and deliberately tripped on the wall of this well, scratching his shin slightly. He told his old cook about this and that because of the danger had decided to fill in the hole. At that time there happened to be some roadworks going on nearby, and each day a horse-drawn cart passed in front of Masaki's property filled with rubble. A noticeboard had been set up asking if anyone wanted any spare earth, so Masaki spoke to the site manager, and for a fee had two loads delivered to his house. The driver brought his cart right into the wild and unkempt garden, dumping the earth into a large pile. He told Masaki he could have some workmen come and fill in the old well any time he wanted - though of course Masaki's intention was to first hurl Fuyuo's corpse to the bottom of that well and cover her up with a little soil so no-one would notice.

So, all the pieces were now in place. All that was left was to decide on a day - though even in this regard Masaki had already made plans. As I mentioned before, Masaki had continued his covert surveillance of Ikeuchi and Fuyuo, and so always knew when and where their next meeting would be. At that time, Fuyuo's show had come to the end of its run, so she would travel from her house to any arranged rendezvous. But on such occasions she would deliberately not book a car from the office, but instead walk to the corner of the main street and pick up a passing cab. Masaki was well aware of this. In truth, it was because he knew of such a habit that he'd decided on including a car in his murderous plot in the first place.

7

It was a cold day in November. The sky had been clear since early morning - the air so bright and fresh the sharp outline of Mount Fuji had been visible from any high vantage point - but when night came a chill wind began to blow and the speckled stars shone with an eerie luminosity. That evening at around seven o'clock, Masaki Aizou's car slipped past the gates of his gloomy mansion, and with a splendid growl, and its twin headlights blazing exultantly, it headed in the direction of Azumabashi Bridge by the embankment of the Sumida river. In the driver's seat Masaki casually held the steering wheel, appearing curiously happy, whistling a tune to himself - *Oh, what a fine evening it was!* - and what a jovial mood Masaki was in. Perhaps this kind of excessive cheer seems unbecoming for someone setting off to commit such a terrible crime. But for Masaki it didn't feel like gruesome murder was his intention that evening. He was going to meet his beloved bride, who for over 10 years he'd been longing for desperately. Tonight he would take complete possession of both the girl he had once worshiped as a goddess, and the body that had haunted his dreams with a delicious torment too much to bear. Nobody could stop him now, not even Ikeuchi Koutarou - *Ah, what delight, it was beyond compare!* - and the crystalline blackness of the night, the sparkling stars, even the breeze that came through the gaps in the windscreen and played against his cheeks, if these were not blessings for their bizarre marriage, what were they?

Fuyuo had arranged to meet Ikeuchi at eight o'clock, so at half past seven Masaki was already in place, parked by a crossroads on the main street where the actress always hailed a ride. In the guise of a shabby cab driver waiting for a fare Masaki crouched down in his seat and pulled his cap over his eyes. A red Tokyo cab sticker stood out on his windscreen - his rear license plate, issued to him by the police, was now switched for a fake, bearing the number of a commercial vehicle. The car would have appeared to anyone as just another Ford awaiting its next passenger.

Just as Masaki was beginning to impatiently wonder if something had happened that night to change their plans - as if this were some kind of signal - Fuyuo suddenly appeared from around the corner. She was dressed in a deliberately plain outfit: a black half-length coat over a brownish kimono, a black shawl covering half her face. As she trotted quickly in his direction - maybe because of the shadow cast by the street lamps - even her complexion seemed drab somehow.

At that moment there were no passing cabs for her to hail, so Fuyuo naturally made her way to Masaki's car. She was of course completely taken in by his deceit.

"Tsukiji, by the Tsukiji third precinct tram stop." Fuyuo hurriedly opened the rear passenger door and slipped inside, directing her instructions at Masaki's back. He remained seated without turning around. His heart sung in triumph as he leaned forward and started the car in the direction he'd been ordered. The route he chose took them through a quiet part of town onto a busy commercial avenue, thronged with lively shops and restaurants. This street was actually a vital part of Masaki's plan. As he drove, he looked up from underneath the peak of his cap at the rear view mirror, keeping an eye on the back passenger seat windows, waiting for a reaction...*any minute now, any minute now*...when shortly, it happened. Just like she did that time half a year ago, Fuyuo pulled down each of the window shades to the side and behind her, to avoid the bright lights of the city (a glass partition covered by a blind separated the driver and rear passengers in box type Fords of this type). Masaki's heart pounded like a small creature raging about inside his chest; his throat dried up as if he'd been on a cross country run; his tongue hardened like a piece of wood in his mouth. But he endured these agonies, and kept on driving.

When he got halfway down the bustling avenue the sound of delirious music could be heard up ahead. It was a band of musicians playing old folk songs and singing roughly at the top of their voices, wildly blaring out the tune to a *Kappore* dance. They were there to draw in customers to a circus that was in town and had set up a large tent on an empty plot of land. In front of the circus a heaving mass of people filled the sidewalk. Anyone passing at that moment would have been completely taken in by the dazzling scene; and the deafening music bellowed above the thundering noise of the roadway, as a torrent of trams, cars, and bicycles poured back and forth. Just as Masaki had anticipated this gave him a secure stage to perform his crime.

He pulled over to the side of the road and suddenly stopped the engine. In a flash he leapt from the driver's seat and into the back of the car, slamming the passenger door shut from the inside. He'd parked right behind a stall selling skewers of grilled chicken, but even if someone had seen him, the shades of the passenger windows were pulled right down, so whatever happened inside was completely hidden. As soon as he'd jumped into the car, he aimed straight for Fuyuo's throat. Soft and white, it writhed pliantly between his hands.

"Forgive me, please forgive me. You were just too beautiful, I couldn't let you live."

Crying incoherently, he squeezed that soft white neck hard enough to break it in two. With the rapid speed of thought of those facing their own death, Fuyuo recognized at once this crazed cab driver was in fact Masaki. But, as though in a nightmare, her whole body felt numb, her tongue cramped in her mouth, and she was powerless to escape or cry for help. She only stared back at him with wide, unblinking eyes, strangely appearing to either laugh or cry, and seeming to thrust her neck forward as if to say, "Here, take it".

Masaki continued to squeeze long after it was necessary to do so. He was afraid if he let go Fuyuo might spring back to life, but even if he wanted to, his fingers had lost all feeling and wouldn't respond to his commands. He couldn't stay that way forever though. Tentatively he relaxed his grip, and like a jellyfish washed up on dry land, his victim limply crumpled in a heap onto the floor of the car.

He lifted the cushions off the seat and with some difficulty managed to fit Fuyuo's body into the box-like space underneath.

He then returned the cushions to their previous position and sat down on them, staying like that for a while to calm himself. Outside the noise of the *Kappore* dance band continued to vigorously ring out. A thought occurred to Masaki and he shuddered suddenly.

What if this was just a trick to put him at ease? What if he raised the shades and there were rows and rows of faces lined up on the street and a thousand eyes staring in at him?

Nervously, he took a peek through a gap in the window, but thankfully not one face was turned his way. People on trams, on bicycles, and walking on the sidewalk, quickly hurried by without paying any interest to his car whatsoever. Realizing he was safe he came to his senses a little. He straightened out his clothes and looked around the car interior for anything he might have missed. It was then he noticed a small handbag hidden by the rubber mat in the seat-well. Of course it was Fuyuo's. When he looked inside there was nothing much of interest - but there was a small pocket mirror, so he opened this up and peered at his own face. Although a little pale, he certainly didn't have the look of a crazed killer. He stared at his reflection for a long time, making an effort to steady his breathing and return his complexion back to normal. When he'd at last composed himself, he suddenly jumped back into the driver's seat and hurriedly drove off, crossing the tram line and returning in the direction he had come. He headed toward a quiet, lonely neighborhood, then stopped the car in front of a shrine he found there. Checking nobody was in sight, he turned off the headlights and quickly raised all the window shades, peeled off the red Tokyo cab sticker and switched the number plate back to the original genuine one. He was now completely calm when he turned the headlights on again and started off home. Feeling very pleased with himself each time he passed a police box he deliberately slowed down and whispered: "I say officer, there's the corpse of a beautiful young woman in the back of my car. And look at me, wouldn't you believe I'm the murderer."

When Masaki arrived home he parked in the garage, made another inspection of himself and the car, then strode through the front door of his house calling to the cook who was in the kitchen.
"I know it's late, but could you run an errand for me? You know the foreign liquor store Tsuruya by the Asakusa *Kaminari* gate, could you go there and get me a good quality bottle of wine, it doesn't matter what kind, whatever you can buy with this." So saying Masaki held out two 10 yen notes to the old woman. Knowing her master didn't drink as a rule the woman pulled a quizzical expression, "Wine, you say?"
"Well, just this once, something has put me in a good mood tonight", Masaki explained, smiling pleasantly. And although he did indeed want something to celebrate with on his peculiar wedding night, his main reason for sending the cook to Asakusa was so he could move Fuyuo's body to the second floor of the old storehouse.
In the half an hour that the old woman was away, Masaki carried his lifeless bride up to his room, and even had time to remove the box-like apparatus he had fitted under the seat of his car and put things back exactly as they had been, thereby concealing the last piece of evidence. Unless someone forced their way into that forbidden storehouse and witnessed Fuyuo's body for themselves, nobody could ever suspect him of anything.
Some time later, the disturbed figure of Masaki Aizou and the corpse of Fuyuo Kinoshita lay face to face on the floor of Masaki's secret room. The reddish brown glow of a single candle illuminated the bride's cold and shamelessly naked body. On the other side of the room, the life-sized wooden Buddhist statues and *Noh* masks made a kind of gruesome, bittersweet contrast. How strange, it seemed to Masaki, that just one hour ago he'd been in awe of this popular actress - so distant or even forbidding if the mood took her, sharp and quick-witted, scornful of the ordinary world - and now her bare cadaver lay right before his eyes, helplessly exposed. It was as though something impossible, that only existed in his dreams, was now reality.

This time, he was the one to feel contempt and pity. Not only could he hold her hand, but touch her cheek, embrace her, or fling her aside, and she would not be able to laugh or sneer like she had that evening. But how wondrous - this woman, Fuyuo Kinoshita, who he'd idolized as a child, who'd been the object of his frantic longing for the last six months, was now entirely his.

Other than the bluish-black strangulation marks around her neck and the pallor of her face she looked almost as she had in life. Though her eyes, wide open, stared emptily into space as if made of glass; her mouth hung slackly, revealing beautiful teeth and the tip of a tongue; and her lips were colorless. Somehow she seemed like one of the life-like dolls shown at the *Hanayashiki* amusement park. If you looked closely at her skin you could see her pores, and a soft downy hair on her arms and thighs, but step back and it appeared sleek and translucent.

The illusory light of the candle made countless soft shadows on her body. The contours of her breasts and stomach were like magnificent sand dunes swelling up, and her whole figure like a strange white mountain range at sunset. Masaki saw a hazy and secretive beauty as he examined every detail, the soaring ridges, the beguiling curves, the mysterious darkness in the smooth, deep, valleys.

Human beings when they are alive, no matter how hard they might try to stay completely still, always give the impression of movement somehow. The dead though are utterly motionless. Although the difference is barely discernible, it is horrifying to behold. Fuyuo was so profoundly silent and inert. While lying exposed in such a slovenly posture she was almost pathetically quiet, like a scolded child.

Masaki took her hand, and as he played with it on his knee he gazed at Fuyuo's face. Her body had not yet started to stiffen so her arm was completely slack, making it very heavy, and her skin still felt warm.

"You are finally mine, sweet Fumiko. However much you scorn or mock me from the other world it doesn't matter now. Because I have your body to do with as I please. I am deaf to your spirit's words, and blind to its looks of reproach."

Masaki addressed Fuyuo's corpse, but just like one of the Hanayashiki dolls she remained silent. There now seemed to be a white film over her vacant eyes, and discreet gray spots appearing at the corners (Masaki hadn't yet guessed at the awful significance of this). Fuyuo's jaw hung open as if she were yawning, and Masaki, feeling a little sorry for her, pushed her chin up with his hand. Although he pressed and pressed, it took some time to get her mouth to stay closed. When her lips were finally squeezed together like thick overlapping petals, precious and desirable, she seemed almost alive again. The sweet gossamer-like flesh of her delightful nostrils, which were widened as though flexed, also held an indefinable charm.

"It's just the two of us now in this whole wide world. We are outcasts, no one will touch us. I've always shied away from the gaze of others, and have now committed the grave sin of murder. And you, well, you live no more. Behind the thick walls of this storehouse we can stay unseen, whisper to each other, and stare into each other's eyes. Does this sound lonely to you? I suppose for someone who lived such a glorious life as yours it may seem rather miserable."

As he said these words a distant memory awoke in Masaki: In the corner of a murky parlor, in an old-fashioned rural home, a shy timid child has built an unbroken wall of wooden blocks around himself. The infant cradles a doll, tears in his eyes, pressing his cheek against the toy's, and muttering to it. Of course this young boy is Masaki Aizou, aged six or seven. But that bashful, whey-faced brat has now grown up, and in place of wooden blocks he has shut himself away in an old storehouse, and in place of that doll, he now mutters to Fuyuo's corpse.

What a strange comparison - when this thought occurred to Masaki the sudden affection he felt for the lifeless body in front of him made his skin prickle. Masaki lifted up Fuyuo's head and pressed her cold cheek against his own, just like how he'd embraced that doll all those years ago. As he held her, his eyelids became hot and swollen, then tears dripped down and he felt them slip along the channel where their cheeks met and towards his jaw.

9

The next morning, when the sky behind the metal grill of the small north-facing window was the bright blue of a late autumn day, Masaki opened his shriveled, yellow eyes - his face blackened with soot - and found himself crumpled at the feet of the Buddhist statue in the corner of the room. Fuyuo's luscious body lay on the tatami, now sadly stiffened with rigor mortis - although this did not make her unattractive, but was instead strangely alluring, like she was some kind of illicit realistic mannequin.

At that moment his exhausted brain began to buzz with a peculiar notion. His plan from the beginning had been to take complete possession of Fuyuo just once - thus fulfilling his murderous ambition - then hide her corpse in the garden's old well that same night. This should have satisfied him, but he now realized he'd miscalculated terribly. He'd never imagined the power his lover's corpse would have over him. Because the life had now gone out of Fuyuo's body it had the lure of a peculiar wilderness. He felt he was sinking endlessly into a bottomless mire, suffocating in its pleasant aroma. This was a desire found only in nightmares and the pits of hell, hence it was fiercer, sweeter, and more deranged than any of this world.

Masaki couldn't bear to part with Fuyuo's cadaver. He couldn't live without her - he had to indulge this strange love forever, just the two of them in their own reality, within the thick walls of this storehouse - no other possibility occurred to him. *Forever*...he contemplated absently. But when the chilling implication behind the word "forever" suddenly struck him, he leapt to his feet in fear and started pacing the room. There was not a moment to lose he thought, but then, no matter how fast he acted, it was perhaps already too late.

A swarm of tiny insects seemed to be crawling over the creases of Masaki's brain...*scratch, scratch, scratch, scratch, scratch, scratch, scratch, scratch, scratch*...devouring everything they came across, the sound of their chewing buzzing in his ears. For a long time he was wracked by indecision, then gingerly, he crouched over his lover's body - now exposed to the morning's harsh light - and made a thorough examination. At first glance there seemed to be little change, other than that rigor mortis now extended across her whole body, increasing the sense of artificiality. But when he looked closer he could see her eyes were ruined: gray spots almost completely covered the whites; the pupils had cloudy cataracts; and the irises looked murky and blurred. Overall they seemed hard and shiny like glass, and lacked all moisture. When he lifted up her hands, he could see her thumbs had bent down towards her palms - as though deformed - and could not be moved.

Masaki turned his gaze to her upper torso. Due to the position her body had been lying in, the flesh around her shoulders had wrinkled and the pores of her skin were strangely enlarged. When Masaki tried to lift her slightly to correct this, his eye was drawn to the part of her back that had been in contact with the tatami mat. He suddenly reeled back in shock at what he saw. Several blue gray specks had already appeared - one of the "marks of death". Like the mysterious phenomenon of rigor mortis, these sores were a prelude to decomposition, the effect after death of obscure microscopic organisms. Masaki had read there were three types of these tiny creatures: those that dwelled in the air; those that lived without air; and amphibious types suited to land and water. What they were exactly, and where they came from was unclear, but like unseen germs they gnawed away at a corpse with frightening speed. These mysterious, invisible bugs were more terrifying than any wild animal.

Masaki grew panicky and restless, as though a flame that he couldn't see was rapidly spreading all around him. He couldn't sit still or stand, then for no reason at all he clattered down the stairs and went into the main house. His cook looked at him curiously, "Are you hungry? Shall I make something?" she asked, but he only muttered he was fine then returned to the front of the storehouse. He locked the door from the outside, rushed back to the main house to get a pair of wooden sandals, then went to the garage to start the car. When the engine had warmed up he jumped into the driver's seat, pulled out of the gates to his property and headed in the direction of Azumabashi bridge.

When he got to the main road he noticed some children playing there had stopped to point at him and laugh. The blood drained from his face in fright, but in the next moment he realized it was because he was still wearing his night clothes. He felt instant relief but acute embarrassment at the same time, and now blushing, he turned the car around.

After changing hurriedly he drove off again, still with no idea where he was going. He traveled aimlessly from neighborhood to neighborhood although his brain was working busily, lost in contemplation of every method of preservation he could think of. *A vacuum? An airtight box? Ice? Salt? Embalming fluids? Creosote? Carbolic acid?* In spite of his speed, he never seemed to get anywhere and just kept going round and round in circles. In one district there was a store with a banner outside with "ICE" written on it, so he stopped the car and entered briskly. Inside was a large ice room painted blue. A woman in her early forties appeared from the back, greeted Masaki curtly and stared at him. When Masaki asked for some ice, she replied wearily "How much?" not expecting a large order.

As he began to speak Masaki's bashfulness snatched the words from his mouth, rephrasing them into something else: "I'd only like a little to cool my head please". When he got back to the car with a small block of ice tied with string he continued his aimless wandering, putting the block on the floor by his feet. The ice had started to melt and soak through the soles of his shoes by the time he came to a large liquor store and noticed an open-topped box about a meter square filled to the brim with salt. He stopped the car again and got out. But instead of salt, for no reason at all he bought a cup of *sake*, and gulped it down as though this had been his intention all along. Masaki now had no idea what he was doing, he restlessly raced from place to place with the vague impression of being pursued. His face flushed hotly from the alcohol he had drunk, and despite the chill in the air, several beads of sweat had broken out on his forehead. All the while he thought about Fuyuo, laid out back at the storehouse, and in this brilliant vision it seemed her naked white flesh was being eaten away, moment by moment, like a fire spreading across her body, and a voice kept murmuring in Masaki's ear. *Do something, do something...*

After more than two hours of aimless driving, Masaki's car finally ran out of gas. He was in a quiet part of town so it took a ridiculous amount of effort to find a gas station and carry a can back to the car. When he finally got moving again, he suddenly thought, as if for the first time, *what am I doing again?* then a moment later, *oh, but I haven't had breakfast yet, I have to hurry home, cook will be waiting*. He asked directions from a boy standing at the side of the road and headed back. It took half an hour before he reached Azumabashi Bridge, but when he got there, he again began to question his actions. Breakfast was now far from his mind, and he slowed the car right down, absorbed in thought. This time though, an idea hit him like a divine revelation. *Why didn't I think of it before?* Masaki angrily admonished himself, but his expression brightened as he changed direction once again. He now headed for the medical instrument shop next to the university hospital in the district of Hongo.

Masaki hesitated for a moment outside the wide shopfront. The store's metal shelves were painted white and filled with an array of unsettling items: shiny silver appliances; vivid red and blue models of the human figure with the skin peeled off. Finally Masaki wandered in, shadow-like, and caught the attention of a young shop assistant. "I need a syringe," he said abruptly, "a large syringe for injecting preservative into the arteries of a dead body."

Although Masaki had tried to make himself very clear the shop assistant seemed rather taken aback and peered at him suspiciously. Masaki's face turned bright red as he repeated himself - he was dressed in his shabby cab driver clothes which the assistant observed disdainfully.

"I've never heard of such a syringe," the man said curtly.

"But you must have. The university uses them. Please go and ask someone else." Masaki stared back at the shop assistant. He was fully prepared for a stand-off with this man. The assistant grudgingly walked off into the back of the shop and after a while the manager, a slightly older man, came out. When Masaki repeated his request, the man looked at him curiously and asked, "What do you intend to use such a thing for?"

"To inject formaldehyde into the arteries of a dead body of course. I know you have one, you can't hide it from me."

The manager grimaced, "You're joking of course. You see, such a hypodermic syringe does indeed exist. But it's an item even the university only orders very occasionally. I'm afraid we don't stock them here in our shop." He spoke politely, pausing between words, as though explaining something to a child. Then he looked pityingly at Masaki's disheveled attire.

"Then sell me a replacement. You have large syringes I suppose? I'll take your largest." Masaki could no longer hear himself speak. Words just seemed to come out of his mouth in a low rumble.

The manager hesitated and scratched his head, "We do have something, but it's a little unconventional, are you sure about this?"

"It's fine. I'll take it. How much do I owe you?" Masaki's hands trembled as he opened up his purse. With no other option the manager sent the young assistant to get the item, then when he returned handed it to Masaki who paid in full. After this Masaki burst out of the shop and drove to a nearby pharmacy where he bought a large amount of embalming fluid, then he hurried homewards.

10

With baited breath and great deal of trepidation Masaki climbed the stairs to the second floor of the storehouse wondering what awful change could have taken place in Fuyuo's body. But to his surprise, when he entered the room she seemed even more beautiful than she had that morning. Although stiff with rigor mortis, her slightly swollen, pallid flesh had a glossy shine, like she was some beguiling cold-blooded creature that lived at the bottom of the sea. Her expression which up till then had been a picture of anguish - with strangely down-turned eyebrows - now seemed as serene as the Virgin Mary's - the corners of her mouth, which Masaki had held shut the night before, now opened slightly revealing white teeth and a slight grin. With vacant cataract-ridden eyes, and a translucent wax-like complexion, she seemed like a marble statue of the smiling Holy Mother.

Masaki felt relieved and slightly foolish for being so anxious earlier. *If only I could capture Fuyuo in this moment for eternity,* he thought, unable to stop himself from entertaining such a vain hope.

Although he had no special medical knowledge, Masaki had read somewhere that the latest and simplest method of embalming was to inject preservative into the body's arteries and force out all the blood. He also recalled a technique for the dilution of embalming fluid. Although extremely apprehensive he set his heart on this procedure. While taking care not to draw the attention of his cook he carried buckets and containers of water from the ground floor up to his room. He then mixed up a solution of formaldehyde and prepared the syringe.

Masaki then spread a large sheet of wax paper underneath Fuyuo's body. While checking with a medical textbook, he gouged at an area between Fuyuo's legs with a razor blade and cut through her main artery. Red blood streamed out of this slippery eel-like tube, and Masaki struggled at first to grab hold of it. His face was now completely white, as though he was the one under the knife, and his breathing ragged. He took the glass body of the syringe without its needle attached, filled it with the preservative solution, and inserted its narrow point into Fuyuo's severed artery. With one hand he held the join closed so no air would escape, and with the other he pressed on the plunger. But perhaps because he'd made some error somewhere this task proved impossible for an amateur like Masaki. However much he pressed, his fingers would simply begin to feel numb, and the solution in the syringe would not go down. Out of frustration he pumped the plunger as hard as he could at rapid intervals, but the solution started to flow backwards and red liquid spilled the other way - and however many times he tried, he got the same result. Like an industrious young schoolboy tinkering with some machine Masaki attempted to tie the seal between the syringe and artery with string; he tried cutting a thick vein near to the artery; he tried everything he could; but just as schoolboys always end up wrecking the machine they are tinkering with, so too Masaki, who only enlarged the wound in Fuyuo's leg. It was around ten o'clock when he finally gave up this futile attempt at surgery - but even so what incredible effort he had put in - since noon that day, he'd been utterly absorbed in his work for almost ten hours.

While disposing of the equipment, cleaning up the sea of blood, and washing himself, Masaki fell into despair and was assailed by a great fatigue. He'd not slept at all the night before, so for two days running he'd been overworking both his mind and body. However thrilling it had been, he'd now exhausted all his energy. Feeling lightheaded he collapsed where he was, and soon began to snore loudly - sleep engulfed him like a black quagmire.

The red flame of a single candle, spluttering as it slowly died out, illuminated the resulting picture of hell: the pathetic figure of Masaki, pale as a ghost, beads of sweat appearing at the tip of his nose, his mouth gaping, sunk in a deathly sleep, while next to him lying in eerie contrast, the seductive form of Fuyuo's white corpse, seemingly floating on air.

11

It was past noon the next day when Masaki awoke. All night, even while asleep, his mind had been in turmoil with a frantic sense of panic. When he finally opened his eyes he lay there blankly, wondering if the last two days had simply been a nightmare. It still felt as if he were dreaming, even with Fuyuo's body lying nearby, and the chemical stench of formaldehyde filling the room mixed with the suffocating bittersweet aroma of death.

But however long he waited it seemed this dream was never going to end - and whether asleep or not he couldn't stay that way forever - so eventually he crawled over to inspect his lover's corpse. When he saw the transformation that had occurred there he was brought back to his senses with a start.

The position of Fuyuo's body had changed completely, as if she'd been tossing and turning in her sleep. Although lifeless, it had up until last night at least maintained a certain resilience, and not given the impression of inanimacy. But now it was as if a thick liquid had solidified into one lump, with nothing of Fuyuo remaining at all. When Masaki touched her flesh it felt soft like tofu, and he realized the stage of rigor mortis had now passed. But more than this, what shocked him most was the profuse number of lead colored blotches that now appeared all over her skin. These irregular shaped death spots were like a monstrous pattern that covered her whole body. With the sureness of the ticking of a clock, the microscopic creatures had steadily devoured more territory, multiplying in their millions, moving unseen. The speed at which these organisms ate away at the flesh was truly remarkable for their infinitesimal size. What was more, there was nothing anyone could do when faced with such violence - you simply had to fold your arms and look on in silence.

Once he'd passed on the opportunity to bury his lover, Masaki had learnt for himself how much more charming the body could be in death than in life, and became the prisoner of a torturous desire. In return for this, he now had to watch on helplessly as his lover's pitiful corporeal form was so slowly but unmistakably eaten away by these bloodcurdling microscopic bugs. He desperately wanted to fight them, but while he could plainly see the awful results of their work, he had no one to fight against. His enemy was invisible. Compelled by the urgency of his situation Masaki considered trying again the method from the day before, but he knew this would be hopeless. Syringes and embalming fluid were beyond him - but using ice or salt was also out of the question - as well as the problem of transporting such bulky raw materials he was averse to the feeling of isolation from Fuyuo these techniques would give. Whatever he tried Masaki was well aware that although he could delay the process of decomposition for a short time he could not stop it completely. Fantastic visions flitted through his fevered mind: a giant glass vacuum; a body encased in a block of ice like the "iced flowers" exhibited at fairs or used as lavish party decorations. He even thought of the store with the dimly lit ice room where he'd felt so intimidated by the woman working there.

In the end though he had to give in - but then another thought occurred to him.

Ah, but what about makeup? I can at least paint over the effects of these awful bugs, so their relentless advance remains unseen.

Although this makeshift approach felt rather defeatist, if there was any way at all to prolong his bizarre love affair - even for a minute or just one second - he had to try it. He rushed out to buy some powdered white pigment and a small brush. When he returned, he made a solution with this powder in a tub of water, then like a master doll maker finishing off one of his life-like creations he applied this whitewash to the whole of Fuyuo's body. Once the grotesque death spots had been covered up he then used regular paint to shade her cheeks pink, draw on eyebrows, turn her lips red, and add some color to the edges of her ears - in the style of an actresses' stage makeup - then he shaded the rest of her body as he saw fit, spending a good five or six hours on this task in all. Although his original intention had been only to hide the gray blotches and darkened patches, Masaki grew strangely fascinated with the process of decoration itself. In the guise of some outlandish artist depicting a seductive nude Masaki moved his brush over Fuyuo's body while murmuring his adoration, even kissing the cold canvas before him as he became more thrilled and engrossed in his work. When he was finally finished the painted corpse had an eerie resemblance to the figure of Salome Masaki had witnessed on stage at the S theater. From the beginning Fuyuo had held an intrinsic beauty, but when covered from head to toe in such vivid makeup she was invested with an even greater allure. Masaki felt it an incredible blessing that her lifeless form, eaten away beyond recovery, could retain such vitality, and indeed a seductive charm beyond that which she'd had in life.

For the next three days there was no great change in Fuyuo's appearance. Other than venturing into the house for meals Masaki spent all this time shut away with his corpse bride, driven to his wit's end by a final longing - weeping madly and howling with laughter - feeling as though his world was coming to an end. Only one brief episode broke the monotony. One afternoon Masaki was woken from a thick muddy sleep by the sound of a wooden rattle. The old cook used this toy instead of a bell to catch his attention when visitors came to the house, so hearing this Masaki - thinking his crime had finally been discovered - suddenly sprang to his feet. He covered Fuyuo's body with some bedding and crept down the stairs. For a moment he waited at the storehouse entrance listening intently, then flung open the heavy door. As he suspected the cook was standing outside. "Young master, Mister Ikeuchi is here to see you" she informed him. Hearing Ikeuchi's name Masaki felt an instant relief, but in the next moment wondered if his friend was now suspicious and had come to check on him. "Did you say I was in?" he asked.

"Ah, yes" the cook replied nervously.

"Never mind. Tell him you went to look for me but I wasn't there and must've gone out without you realizing. Then for the time being whoever comes to the house say I'm not in." Masaki gave his instructions then closed the door without another word. A little while later though he regretted not meeting Ikeuchi. If he'd only had the courage to see his friend he could have found out the purpose of his visit. Because he'd avoided him Masaki now could only wonder at Ikeuchi's intentions. This left him fretting over the situation. All kinds of thoughts ran through his mind as he sat in that silent room beside Fuyuo's speechless corpse, his unease slowly increasing into something monstrous. He became assailed by a terrible dread, but all he could do to dispel this fear was absently caress the gaudily painted body before him, like a philanderer still intoxicated by the previous night's debauchery.

12

This three day respite was not to last however, and calamity lay ahead. Although there was no great change in Fuyuo's appearance - and in fact just like how a candle burns with a uniquely dazzling flame just before going out, her strange makeup made her more ravishing than she'd been in life - beneath this superficial calm the loathsome creatures had continued their work. Millions of tiny jaws had chewed away at Fuyuo's insides, devouring her innards. Then one morning Masaki awoke from a long sleep to see a terrible transformation in his lover, and almost let out a shriek of terror. Where only the night before his beautiful bride had lain beside him, there was now the white, bloated figure of what appeared to be a female Sumo wrestler. Fuyuo had inflated like a rubber ball. Countless cracks had opened up in the whitewash over her body, like the fissures in the glaze of *Soma* pottery, and between the gaps in this grotesque mesh patches of brown colored skin could be seen. Her face had also become distended, so now it was like that of a monstrous cherubic baby.

Masaki had read about this phenomenon. After death, the unseen microbes break down the walls of the intestines, penetrating the blood vessels and peritoneum, discharging a gas. A process of liquidation also begins, but it is the force of the swelling that is most noticeable. Not only does the body expand to a gigantic size, the diaphragm is squeezed up towards the top of the rib cage, and at the same time blood from deep within the cadaver is forced out through the surface of the skin, a curious event that is perhaps responsible for the birth of the vampire legend.

The end had finally come. Once Fuyuo's body swelled to its limit, next would be the stage of putrefaction. Her skin and muscles would turn to a viscous liquid and simply leak away. Like a threatened child Masaki looked around wildly, his eyes glistening, his face screwed up as though at any minute he would burst into tears. For a long time he stayed like this until suddenly a thought struck him. He leapt to his feet and hurried over to the bookshelf where he pulled out a single dogeared volume. On the spine of this book was written the words "Egyptian Mummies". Although he knew full well this would be of no use to him now, he desperately flicked through the pages as if his lover's life depended on it. In a madly vexatious mood he finally came to the following passage:

The most effective method of mummification is this: First make a deep incision under the ribs on the left side and through this wound draw out all internal organs leaving only the heart and kidneys. Then insert a curved metal tool into the nostril and extract every last trace of the cerebral matter. Rinse the hollowed out skull and torso with palm wine, then inject myrrh and other medicines through the nasal cavity into the cranium. Fill the abdomen with dried fruit and stitch up the opening. After soaking the entire body for seventy days in a soda ash solution, remove and carefully wrap in hemp cloth sealed with resin.

Masaki read this section several times then seemingly on the verge of hurling the book to the floor instead stared vacantly into space, tapping his head with his fists, muttering to himself "what was it, what was it again?" like a senile old man desperately trying to recall his own name. Suddenly he rushed down the stairs as though remembering an urgent errand and hurried out of the storehouse. With no destination in mind he left the gates of his property walking quickly in the direction of the Sumida embankment. When he got there the turbid water of that great river seemed like an endless swarm of squirming insects, and he felt as if the ground beneath him was covered in a blanket of creeping microorganisms, leaving him with nowhere to step. Nevertheless he walked on, repeating out loud again and again "There must be something I can do, there must be something" his anguish now plain for all to see. At one point he almost cried out for help and had to bite his tongue to stop himself. He continued this aimless wandering for half an hour, then lost in introspection he was careless in his footing and tripped on a small rock, falling to the ground with a thud. Although not hurt, a peculiar change came over Masaki. Instead of getting back to his feet he lowered his head further and began to crawl about in the dirt, groveling pathetically to whoever approached him. This was such a strange sight a crowd soon gathered, catching the eye of a passing constable. This policeman, feeling some sympathy for Masaki, helped him up and asked his address, then accompanied him back to Azumabashi bridge thinking Masaki had been struck by some kind of lunacy. As they walked together Masaki blurted out his confession: "Officer, did you know a cruel murder had recently taken place? I say cruel because the victim in this case was such a pure and innocent angel. But then the murderer, a soft-hearted fool, was himself a good person. It makes no sense right? Anyway, I know where the body of that angel now lies. Would you like me to tell you? Officer? Would you?" Masaki repeated himself several times but the policeman only laughed and paid no attention to his incoherent raving.

Some time later, after Masaki had not appeared for his meals for two whole days, the old cook contacted the leaseholder of the property. They made a report to the police station and two officers came and broke down the door to Masaki's forbidden storehouse. A suffocating stench of death filled the room on the second floor, and in the dim light two bodies could be seen, covered in a mass of maggots. The first body was immediately identified as Masaki Aizou, the protagonist of our story, but it took some time to confirm the second body as that of the missing actress Fuyuo Kinoshita. Her remains were in a much later stage of decomposition, added to which her stomach had been mercilessly cut open, causing a trail of festering guts to spill out horribly. Masaki had died with his face thrust downwards into these exposed intestines, and it appeared in his death throes his twisted fingers had dug deeply and vindictively into his lover's putrid flesh.